SKIBIDI TOILET

FRACTURED SIGNALS

FRACTURED SIGNALS

BY LYNDSAY ELY

SCHOLASTIC INC.

If you purchased this book without a cover, you should be aware that
this book is stolen property. It was reported as "unsold and destroyed"
to the publisher, and neither the author nor the publisher has
received any payment for this "stripped book."

SKIBIDI TOILET is a trademark of Invisible Narratives, LLC.
© 2026 Invisible Narratives, LLC. All rights reserved.

All rights reserved. Published by Scholastic Inc., *Publishers since 1920*. SCHOLASTIC
and associated logos are trademarks and/or registered trademarks of Scholastic Inc.

The publisher does not have any control over and does not assume any
responsibility for author or third-party websites or their content.

No part of this publication may be reproduced, stored in a retrieval system,
or transmitted in any form or by any means, electronic, mechanical,
photocopying, recording, or otherwise, or used to train any artificial
intelligence technologies, without written permission of the publisher.
For information regarding permission, write to Scholastic Inc.,
Attention: Permissions Department, 557 Broadway, New York, NY 10012.

This book is a work of fiction. Names, characters, places, and incidents are
either the product of the author's imagination or are used fictitiously, and any
resemblance to actual persons, living or dead, business establishments, events, or
locales is entirely coincidental.

ISBN 979-8-225-01233-5

10 9 8 7 6 5 4 3 2 1   26 27 28 29 30

Printed in the U.S.A.   40

First printing 2026

Book design by Martha Maynard

SKIBIDI TOILET

FRACTURED SIGNALS

PART 1:

BROKEN ALLIANCE

The Skibidi Toilet invasion came quickly and seemingly out of nowhere. By the time the alien threat was fully understood, it had already spread across the Earth, wiping out most of humanity. The Cameramen have led the way in fighting back, but territory continues to be lost at a concerning pace, despite influxes of additional recruits. Without additional resources—and more troops—it won't be long before Earth falls entirely.

IT WAS CLEAR THAT SOMETHING WAS WRONG. There weren't supposed to be this many of them. Not in this part of the city. Not now.

The evening shadows felt like weak cover in the alley where the squad crouched, watching silently as wave after wave of Skibidi Toilets passed by on the street only steps away, sweeping the area for their Cameramen foes. The seemingly endless horde was made up of ordinary grunts for the most part, their grotesque not-quite-human heads extending out of dingy white bowls. But there was the occasional Strider Toilet as well, scrambling across the squad's narrow field of view on its spidery, needle-like legs.

A hand touched his arm in warning. He looked over at his fellow Cameraman, who, like him, was another brand-new recruit to this squad, along with the Camerawoman crouched with them behind a cluster of old trash bins. Their white CCTV Camera heads stayed frozen in anticipation. The trio were recent enough additions that they hadn't yet had a chance to shed the metal ID bracelets that had granted them access to their nearby base; the bracelet of the Cameraman who'd nudged him peeked out from beneath the cuff of his long black coat. C-R-K5L, it said. The Camerawoman's read C-R-De4; he'd seen it earlier when they were back at base, preparing for what was supposed to be a routine, low-conflict patrol. *C* for Cameraman, *R* for the enrollment center they'd come through, and then an individual designation code. His code was 3Dd, though they probably wouldn't need the ID tags much longer, now that they were registered with the base systems.

K5L pointed. 3Dd looked down to find the tip of his foot sticking out beyond the edge of a trash bin. Quickly he pulled it back, out of view. The movement drew the attention of their squad leader, Zero, across the alley behind a pile of debris. She looked up sharply, her intense stare burning into 3Dd as she brought a single finger up in front of her lens.

Quiet!

3Dd withered. One day with this squad and already he was getting scolded for making mistakes. And Zero wasn't known for having anyone on her team that couldn't cut it. He'd be lucky if he wasn't reassigned the moment they got back to base.

Assuming they made it back.

The wave of Toilets seemed never-ending. 3Dd had stopped trying to keep count long ago, and still they slid steadily by the alley entrance. Thankfully they didn't seem interested in the narrow trash-strewn alley. As long as the squad was able to stay out of sight and keep quiet, they would be able to wait it out until the invaders were gone, then sneak away under the cover of darkness.

A scraping sound came from somewhere nearby.

Zero's head whipped around again. 3Dd started to throw his hands up in innocence when a flash of movement from above caught his attention. He looked up just in time to see a Strider Toilet skittering down the brick wall at his back, heading directly for him. 3Dd froze as it leapt, too surprised to react, but an instant before the Strider reached him, a dark shape collided with it.

Zero! She and the Strider crashed into a pile of rotten wooden pallets, fists and spindly legs flying. The squad leader pummeled the Strider Toilet relentlessly, going for its flusher again and again, but the Strider always managed to twist away right before she could grasp it.

De4 pushed past 3Dd, her hands flailing in frustration. *Why aren't you helping?* She shoved her way into the fray, grabbing the Strider Toilet's flusher and yanking on it. The Strider's features switched from rage to terror a moment before its head spiraled into the bowl and disappeared. 3Dd dropped his shoulders in relief—why *hadn't* he done something?—as Zero jabbed a finger toward the mouth of the alleyway.

The skirmish had drawn attention . . . a lot of it. A dozen Skibidi Toilets peered down the alley at them, all jostling for a spot at the front of the pack, their faces warped with rage. Zero signaled. In an instant, the rest of the squad was on their feet and grabbing anything that might be used as a weapon: discarded bricks, wooden planks, old metal piping. Waiting out the Toilet swarm was no longer an option; they were going to have to fight their way free. Zero took the lead, pausing for a moment to make an O shape with one hand. *Zero toilets left alive.* That simple, forceful gesture dictated the squad's philosophy, not to mention earned its leader her name, the number also painted in dark red on the back of her black leather jacket.

It was easier said than done though. 3Dd was at the rear of the squad as they surged forward from their hiding place, throwing themselves at the Toilet invaders. Clearly the Toilets didn't expect that level of fervent resistance; the enemy line broke almost immediately, spilling the battle out of the alley. 3Dd slipped between De4 and K5L, both engaged with Toilets, their fists pounding relentlessly at the fleshy, toothy faces. He grabbed a flusher as he passed, taking out K5L's toilet. His comrade threw a grateful thumbs-up, but 3Dd didn't have a chance to return it. A Toilet knocked his feet out from under him, sending him slamming into the pavement. 3Dd kicked at it, rolling away before the Toilet could attack again, then got back to his feet. The Toilet was on him almost immediately though; he barely managed a punch that connected between its eyes, stunning the foe. Then 3Dd grabbed its flusher. With a piercing death scream, the head spun into the depths of its bowl. De4, her back to him, had taken out her first Toilet too but was already tangling with another opponent. Meanwhile, Zero was caught between two Toilets, holding her own as she swung a rusty pipe at them. As 3Dd waffled about which Camerawoman to assist, another Toilet came at him, but he sidestepped it deftly and yanked the flusher.

Three down! He pumped a fist, his blunder in the alley forgotten. This was his first battle and he'd already taken down several of the enemy. But those triumphant feelings disappeared as K5L stumbled into him, spinning 3Dd around. Suddenly dozens of Skibidi Toilets filled his view, blanketing the street like an infestation of white porcelain bugs.

And yet, K5L clapped him confidently on his shoulder. *Doesn't matter,* the gesture said. *We can take them.*

Hopefully. But 3Dd stood a little straighter as De4 appeared at his side as well. She tossed her head in an unconcerned gesture, balled her fists, and took off at a run. They both followed; they weren't about to be shown up. It didn't matter how many Toilets there were. This was what they'd been trained for, what they were meant to do—take down every porcelain invader that crossed their path.

Like their squad leader had ordered: *Zero Toilets left alive.*

3Dd punched the first Toilet that reached him so hard that its head snapped back, cracking the porcelain behind it. Not that the attacker ever had a chance to realize it; he flushed it before moving on to his next target. Punch, flush, punch, dodge, flush . . . It was an invigorating rhythm, and he savored every scream of surprise and anger as he flushed Toilet after Toilet after Toilet. The others did the same, their squad coming together to cut a path of destruction down the street. 3Dd had felt a surge of pride when he'd been assigned to Zero's group, knowing their reputation, but they were even tougher than he'd expected, leaving the shadowy city street littered with the Toilet dead.

Served the invaders right for being where they weren't supposed to be. This patrol was supposed to be routine—this section of the city clear and quiet according to the briefing they'd had earlier. The squad was to sweep the area and take down whatever odd Skibidi infantry they came across. Encountering a small army of Toilets hadn't been expected, but clearly if they wanted to make a fight of it, the squad was happy to oblige. Face after face crumpled, spun, and flushed, until 3Dd no longer knew how many he'd taken out. What was the point of keeping count anyway? Zero was the only number that mattered.

Speaking of which, 3Dd had lost track of the squad leader, but Zero suddenly sprinted into view, kicking a Toilet into the wall of a nearby building, then following that with a blow across its face with her metal pipe. The force of it was so intense that the Toilet slumped to the ground and didn't move again. Zero spun to find a new opponent and spotted 3Dd. She gave him a cheeky shrug. *No big deal.* The squad leader followed that with a flushing gesture. *One or one hundred, they all flush the same way.*

Of course. Zero hadn't been bothered by what seemed like an endless army of Toilets when they were hiding in the alley, and she wasn't now that they were fighting them head on. Her confidence was contagious. The rush of battle building in him again, 3Dd looked around for the closest Toilet, ready to flush another one into oblivion. But the grunts near him had paused their advance and were looking into the distance, behind 3Dd.

Suddenly an explosion rattled in the distance, felt as much as heard, as the ground beneath them trembled violently. 3Dd turned toward the direction it had come from, down another street that passed between a pair of glassy skyscrapers. Smoke filled the space between them, gray clouds that stood out from the dark of night, as bits of debris fluttered in the air.

3Dd looked at Zero. *An attack? Is it our side or theirs?*

But Zero wasn't paying attention to him. From her intense, concentrated stance, it was clear that she was transmitting what she was seeing via her camera. Strange since, from what he'd heard, Zero preferred to leave that particular task to the other Cameramen and remain focused on fighting. Which meant that whatever was happening, it was important enough that she wanted to make sure their base saw it.

3Dd turned back to the smoke cloud just in time to understand why. Something huge—three stories high at least—was emerging from it. 3Dd took a step back. He didn't mean to, but before this moment, he'd only ever seen the Giant Skibidi Toilets on a monitor, broadcasted by the Cameramen who were unlucky enough to encounter them in battle. They'd looked big then, but in real life . . . What bore down on them was a massive, monstrous incarnation of the smaller Toilet grunts he'd been taking down, with a porcelain exterior white as bone, a vicious grin, and intense, manic eyes that swept over the ensuing conflict. It uttered a string of the Toilets' strange alien words, the deep tones of its voice echoing off the buildings. 3Dd couldn't help it; he began to tremble. There weren't enough of them. There was no way their small solo squad could hope to take out a Giant Toilet like this, not with so many of its smaller counterparts still left to help thwart any attempt at attack.

They needed to retreat.

As he took another fearful step back, Zero's hand clamped down on his shoulder. She wasn't going anywhere. With her other hand, she gestured to De4 and K5L, the two squad members closest. *Follow me!*

3Dd hesitated, but Zero was their leader, and she was giving him a direct order. To his surprise though, she led the trio *away* from the incoming Giant Toilet, instead of toward it. He risked a glance back as they moved; the rest of the squad was still fighting, but they'd begun to fall back as the behemoth Toilet bore down on them, recognizing their clear disadvantage. 3Dd's confusion only deepened as Zero led them back down the alley. Did she think they could hide again? As soon as that thing reached them, they'd be spotted and trapped.

But Zero sprinted to the ladder that hung from a fire escape above, scaling it up to the first landing and waving for the others to follow. De4 didn't hesitate. Neither did K5L. Once again, 3Dd brought up the rear, trailing as they ran up the rusted steps of the precariously built metal structure, headed for the building's roof. And not a moment too soon. Below, smoke from the Toilets' attack had begun to fill the alley, making it hard to see. 3Dd could only hope the rest of the squad was using the foggy haze to their advantage.

3Dd reached the roof and pulled himself onto it, staying low like his companions as they crept over to the edge of the building. It was a solid vantage point for observing the battle below, even if the smoke meant they could only see vague shapes. 3Dd could just make out the taller, leaner figures of the Cameramen interwoven with their chunkier Toilet opponents, trading blows and yanking flushers. They were doing well holding off the advance but were clearly out-numbered. It was only a matter of time before the rest of the squad would be overrun.

Suddenly De4 pointed excitedly. Down the street, in the opposite direction that the Giant Toilet was moving, more Cameramen appeared—dozens of them, all running toward the fight with fists and weapons raised.

Zero slapped a hand on the building's ledge with passion. *Now we've got a chance.* But she directed their attention back toward the Giant Toilet. Reinforcements were great, but they still needed to deal with that not-so-little problem. Zero pointed to herself, the three squad members, and then again toward the Giant Toilet. Drawn by the fresh wave of Cameramen, it was moving faster now, not seeming to care that the new arrivals were better armed than the squad it had already encountered. One of the approaching Cameramen heaved a missile launcher onto one shoulder and fired. Their aim was good, but the Giant Toilet anticipated the attack, shifting at the last moment. The missile caught the edge of the Toilet's tank and exploded, sending white chips into the air, but the damage was minimal, doing nothing to slow the monster down.

K5L threw his hands up with frustration, but Zero waved off his reaction and pointed again. It was up to them. She closed her hand into a fist. *Get ready.*

3Dd went tight all over as the quartet crouched behind the edge of the building, waiting for the moment to make their move. For all that he'd been pumped up while fighting the grunt Toilets, a Giant Toilet was completely different. A punch wasn't going to stun it. They'd have to move fast, go right for the flusher and yank it, all before the massive Toilet had a chance to retaliate. *Relax,* he told himself. He'd seen his fellow Cameramen take down Giants before. It wasn't easy, but it also wasn't impossible. With the new Cameramen reinforcements distracting it—and if they kept their cool and worked as a team—they might just manage to end the day triumphant.

The Giant Toilet drew closer. Again, Zero raised a hand, palm flat, urging patience. Seconds felt like hours as the distinctive scrape of porcelain against asphalt grew louder and louder, punctuated by more explosions in the distance.

Zero tensed. Then she swept her hand down, making a cutting motion in the air. *Go!*

This time, 3Dd didn't hesitate. In unison, all four of them climbed onto the ledge of the building and jumped. The gut-wrenching drag of gravity was quickly followed by limb-rattling impact as the squad landed in a cluster on the tank of the Giant Toilet. 3Dd straightened quickly, taking stock of his surroundings. The air was still hazy, but he could see that they'd all landed safely—De4 and K5L only steps from him and Zero a little farther away, closest to the flusher. She went for it immediately. 3Dd started to move—she'd need help—but the world suddenly pitched. He went flying, landing sharply on one shoulder and then rolling, out of control. The Toilet rushed toward him. He flailed, desperate to arrest his movement as his hand caught something—a ridge of broken porcelain from where the missile had hit. Zero wasn't so lucky. Below her was only a slick whiteness. She slid toward the edge of the Toilet's tank, nothing to stop her. 3Dd lunged, barely catching her by one wrist, but the momentum was still with the squad leader. For an instant, it felt as if they'd both plummet to the street below. Then Zero kicked at the bucking porcelain, pulling herself back onto the tank. Shaky, and still gripping 3Dd's hand, she pulled him up onto his feet.

But the Giant Toilet was not happy about its uninvited guests. It jumped again and shook violently, desperate to throw them off. On the other side of the tank, De4 and K5L were on their stomachs, doing their best to keep from being thrown off.

Hold on! 3Dd tried to move toward them, but the Giant Toilet bucked again, sending him and Zero to their knees. The flusher was close; they were able to catch themselves on the edge of it, regaining their balance. But De4 and K5L had nothing to grab on to. Time slowed again, creeping painfully as he watched his companions tumble to the edge of the Giant Toilet's tank and over it.

No! Fighting to keep from joining them, 3Dd scrambled to the Toilet's edge. A horrible sight awaited: the pair, sprawled on the asphalt below. It was a long fall. Still, he could see De4 move an arm, and K5L's head swiveled from one side to another. Then the Giant Toilet shifted course and the two Cameramen disappeared, crushed beneath it.

3Dd couldn't move. One moment they were there, the next . . . gone. A chill shivered through him. It . . . it wasn't fair. This was the first mission for all three of them. It was supposed to be simple. They should have been celebrating later, back at base. Instead, his friends were dead.

A hand spun him around—Zero, a determined set to her stance. *What are you doing?* She jabbed a finger toward the flusher. *This isn't over yet.*

No, it wasn't. And De4 and K5L weren't the only ones who wouldn't make it back to base if they didn't do something about the Giant Toilet, and quick. Hot with rage and loss, 3Dd felt as if his limbs had turned to cement. It was Zero's indomitable energy that got him moving, her reckless abandon about the only thing that would get them out of this mess now. 3Dd followed her lead, again going for the flusher as the monster beneath them steadied. *It thinks it shook us all off,* 3Dd thought. *Now's our chance.*

Suddenly the Toilet's giant head rose up, slowly and deliberately spiraling their way.

Shoot. Its vicious white teeth snapped, so close that 3Dd felt the edge of his jacket snag as he jumped back. The head went for him again, barely missing, and then attacked Zero, who managed to roll out of the way. The Giant Toilet screeched with frustration, but as rancorous as it was, its position was awkward. As the head twisted, trying for another angle of attack, Zero lunged once again for the flusher, tantalizingly close. This time, it wasn't the Giant Toilet that intercepted her, but a skittering form that clipped Zero and nearly sent her careening off the edge of the tank again. Another Strider Toilet, insect-quick on its spidery appendages as it jumped in to defend the Giant Toilet.

3Dd looked around. *Where the heck had it come from?* Then two more appeared, leaping down from the surrounding buildings. They must be camped out on the rooftops, like the one that had almost ambushed him in the alley. He dodged the first's attack, kicking it off the edge of the Giant Toilet. The other circled more cautiously as the Strider who'd cut Zero off squared up against her again. She threw a punch. The Strider let out a cry as it connected, briefly distracting the one who stood before 3Dd. Not wasting the opening, he threw himself at it. There was a crunch as his fist connected with its ghastly grin. Rattled, the Strider tried to stumble back, but 3Dd grabbed one of its legs, snapping it off at a joint. It wasn't the best weapon, but it was something. Wielding the metal limb like a knife, he stabbed at the Strider, who dodged each attack clumsily. It was so off balance that 3Dd knew all it would take was the right moment, the right opening . . .

He was so focused on the Strider that he barely reacted in time when the Giant's head appeared again, rearing up for a new strike. The Striders had been a calculated attack, he realized, a distraction. Well, it wasn't going to work. As the gaping maw of the Giant Toilet head came at 3Dd, snapping, he grabbed the Strider and pulled it in front of him. The Strider screamed as the Giant's teeth chomped down, a sound quickly cut short.

But there was no time to savor small victories. Zero was still engaged with the Strider attacking her. Its needlelike appendages struck again and again, quick as stinging bees. Zero avoided the attacks with impeccable grace, but her footing kept getting thrown off by the movements of the Giant Toilet. One spidery leg finally landed a blow, sinking deep into her lower leg. She stumbled but didn't fall. Her persistence couldn't last though. Either she'd be bucked off the Giant Toilet with the next lurch or the Strider would finish what it started. Clutching the broken appendage in his fist, 3Dd lunged at the Strider, plunging the metal point deep into its neck. It let out a sound that could only be described as pure rage, but he kept stabbing, again and again. Blood sprayed from the wound, blanketing him, but he didn't stop until the Strider Toilet went limp. Then with Zero's help, he shoved it off the edge of the Giant's tank.

No stopping. No thinking. He didn't need Zero's instruction at this point. The porcelain surface now slick with red, they fought their way across the tank as the Giant's head reared up once more, its teeth like guillotine blades, alien breath as hot and damp as sewage. But they reached the flusher. Working in unison, they grabbed it and yanked.

The roar that followed was second in volume only to the beautiful flushing sound that began. The Giant Toilet head stretched even higher, elongating gruesomely, features contorting as it began to spin round and round. Then it disappeared from their view as the monster was rapidly suctioned into the depths of its own body.

Finally the alien behemoth went still.

3Dd looked up at Zero. She looked back at him. Then, a little shakily, the squad leader gave him a thumbs-up. They'd done it. It had come at a high cost, but they'd stopped the Giant Toilet.

And yet, they were far from safe.

Carnage littered the street below. Bodies lay everywhere, more Toilets than Cameramen, but the Toilet grunts were still coming in droves. There were fewer of the Cameramen reinforcements standing than 3Dd liked, though the ones that remained still fought on valiantly.

Zero turned back to 3Dd. Shook her head.

I know. He nodded, understanding the gesture was for whatever remained of the rest of the squad. *They aren't coming.*

Around them, the Skibidi Toilets were becoming even more agitated as they realized that their champion had fallen, and that the enemies who'd killed the Giant Toilet were still alive but also well within reach of revenge. The grunt Toilets closed in as more

Striders appeared on the building rooftops, dancing on their insect legs with angry impatience. Zero took in the approaching enemy and tipped her camera head with calm consideration, once again broadcasting to whomever was watching. Then she shook herself, rolled her shoulders to loosen them, and stood up straight, ready. Not defeated, not her.

3Dd saw the question in her movements and nodded twice, in quick succession. *Like you even had to ask.*

She gave him another thumbs-up. Then without an ounce of reluctance, she jumped from the defeated behemoth, knocking off several of the smaller Toilets scaling it on her way down.

3Dd watched with admiration until the spindly legs of another Strider appeared over the edge of the tank nearby. Following Zero's lead, he slammed into it and they went flying, plummeting to the street, where the Toilet crunched under 3Dd's weight. That wasn't enough. De4 was dead. So was K5L. As the desire for vengeance took him, he punched, fists flying. *Crunch. Crunch. CRUNCH.* More blood splattered him, the Strider long gone before he was forced to stop pummeling it by the approach of another Toilet. One flush and it was taken care of; two more fell beneath the rebar rod he snatched from the debris on the street. Explosions roared nearby, but he didn't pause to evaluate where they were coming from, or who was causing them. There were too many Toilets, seemingly hundreds, coming from all angles. And he wanted them all *dead*.

Cold focus gripped as he took down one after another, ignoring when a Strider leg punctured his side, or when a grunt collided with his hand, knocking the metal bar from it and leaving him reliant on fists. That was enough for 3Dd. Weapons or no, if his first day in the war was the day he was going to go down, then he was going to go down fighting. Let any of the other Cameramen watching know that they should do the same, that they shouldn't give up, even if the only thing they could see was an insurmountable number of the enemy. Zero was gone, lost in the frenzy. And everywhere, Skibidi Toilets, an endless sea of frenzied alien faces, getting closer and closer until . . .

One of the Toilets knocked 3Dd to the ground. He tried to get up, knew it was all over if he didn't, but another slammed him into the street again. He managed to roll, get on his back, but it was just in time for the Toilet to land on him again, the weight of it heavy enough to pin him down but not merciful enough to crush him. Instead, all he could do was look up into the hysterical, human-but-not-human face, more teeth than anything else as it grinned in triumph. It hooted out a brief, almost mocking noise in its alien language, followed by a laugh. 3Dd tried to shove it off him, but it was useless. And from the way the Toilet's amusement disappeared and its eyes narrowed as it glared down at him, it knew it too.

A flush sounded. Suddenly the face balked with surprise before spinning and disappearing into its bowl. Something heaved the dead Toilet off 3Dd, and a gloved hand appeared, reaching for him. It wasn't one of his squad though, or even another Cameraman.

3Dd had heard the gossip. Been told they'd joined the fight. But this was the first time he'd ever seen a Speakerman in the metallic flesh—entirely relaxed, as if there weren't a dozen more Toilets only moments away from descending on them. He was taller than 3Dd, with a boxy black speaker head accented by little silver spikes set along its top edge. These glinted as the Speakerman nodded at 3Dd and pulled him onto his feet. Around them, the battle was still raging, fought by both Cameramen and Speakermen now, though the ratio of humanoids to Toilets still appeared wildly unbalanced. But the Speakerman's demeanor didn't change. With relaxed, deliberate movements, the Speakerman tossed 3Dd a pair of headphones, motioning to put them on. 3Dd obeyed. The conflict around him dampened audibly, if not physically. Meanwhile, the Speakerman readied himself. Then . . .

The attack his rescuer let loose turned the world into a thick, almost gelatinous riot of sound and vibration. The Toilets nearby shrieked, a sound 3Dd couldn't hear but saw in their horrified features as they were assaulted by it. Then, as quickly as it had begun, it was over. The Toilets dropped, heads lolling back and lifeless. 3Dd felt more of the heavy, buzzing attacks taking place nearby, vibrating the very ground he stood on. As 3Dd moved out from the shadow of the fallen Giant Toilet, he saw that dead Toilets practically blanketed the street, only a few still moving. Cameramen moved toward those that did, dispatching them quickly.

What had been a furious battle only moments before was now suddenly quieted, allowing 3Dd a chance to consider his new ally. Unsure, he took the Speakerman in. Like many of the others, he wore a black suit with a dark gray shirt underneath, accented with a crimson tie. The metal points appeared to be a unique feature. But before 3Dd could consider this further, a familiar figure limped into view.

Zero. She was battered—her coat torn and her lens sporting a new hairline crack—but she was alive. So were a few of the rest of the squad. One by one, they gathered to her, re-forming a semblance of the group they'd started as in the alley. A somber understanding grew as it became clear how many spots were empty—including two of their latest recruits—but now wasn't the time to mourn who'd fallen. That would come later, once they made it safely back to base and had time to attend to injuries. And there were plenty of those. 3Dd pressed a hand to his side where the Strider leg had stabbed him. It wasn't pretty, but it could be repaired. Another of the squad was missing a hand. A third, her whole arm. The Cameramen who had initially reinforced them had taken their share of battle damage as well; the ones still able-bodied combed among the chaos, picking out those comrades who were still alive but unable to do much more than lie where they'd fallen.

Zero clapped him once on the shoulder, squeezing it briefly. 3Dd understood: Despite the losses, they'd come out ahead today. And more so, he'd proven himself as a new member of the squad. He was one of them now. At the beginning of the day, that was all he had wanted. Now something more momentous was taking place. He turned back to the Speakerman who'd saved his life. If it hadn't been for these new allies, none of the squad would have made it.

The Speakerman suddenly pointed at 3Dd's shirt. 3Dd looked down at the Skibidi Toilet blood soaking it, then shrugged. He'd clean it up later. But the Speakerman pointed again, and then at 3Dd's wrist, back and forth. Bloody red shirt. Wrist. Bloody red shirt. Wrist.

Finally 3Dd realized what the Speakerman was actually pointing at: his designation bracelet, which had slipped out of his jacket sleeve. Like 3Dd, it had taken a beating during the fight. The first letter had been scratched off, so that it now spelled out: R-3Dd.

"*Red all over.*" The Speakerman's words were buzzy but clear. "*Redd.*"

Zero threw her head back with amusement and gave the Speakerman a thumbs-up.

Redd. A new name, earned on his first day. It was enough to make one want to break out into a celebratory dance. But Redd—he liked the moniker the moment he attached it to himself—kept it cool. The squad was watching, after all. Instead, he held out a hand in thanks. A moment later, the Speakerman shook it, and Redd understood something new, something pivotal: that the Cameramen were no longer merely a rebellion against the Skibidi Toilet invasion.

Now they were part of an alliance.

THE SKIBIDI TOILET LURCHED FORWARD SO suddenly and with such viciousness that the closest Cameraman jumped back in fear and tripped, falling right onto his backside. Around him, the others began to laugh, the Cameramen with silent heaves, the Speakermen with the low, amused pulse that Redd had become familiar with. He didn't join in, instead going over to the fallen Cameraman and offering him a hand. At first, the Cameraman waved him away, embarrassed, but Redd insisted. Neither of them was a seasoned veteran in this war; it was still natural to carry a modicum of fear. Smart, even. Eventually the hand was accepted and Redd pulled the new recruit to his feet. As he did, a horn sounded.

It came from Zero. She stood above them on the raised walkway that ran around the exterior of the training room. *This is not a game,* her stance said.

The group's joviality disappeared.

The Toilet, however, did not. It still lunged at them, snapping and straining against the chains that kept it tethered to the floor. There were a dozen more like it restrained around the room, all captured during a recent conflict, all for the benefit of the Alliance training that was taking place. It was a little unnerving, Redd thought, having the Toilets within their base—what if one of them got out, reported back on what they saw?—but he had to admit, it was way more satisfying than working with the decoys from training.

Up above, Zero gave the signal to begin the exercise again. Redd fell back into position, the spooked Cameraman to one side of him, a Speakerman in front of him. That Speakerman turned and tipped his head cockily at Redd, metal additions glinting. Spike, as Redd had come to know him, was turning out to be a solid fighting companion, often accompanying Zero's replenished squad on their patrols and reconnaissance missions. He was also seriously fun to hang out with when they'd finished with the hours of drills and maintenance. True, the music he liked to blast from his speaker was louder, grittier, and, well, more *metallic* than the chill tunes the rest of the Speakermen seemed to prefer, but Redd was becoming accustomed to it. It matched Spike's enthusiastic energy and big presence.

But the Speakerman was all business now. He planted his feet, gesturing at the Cameramen behind him to prepare. One by one, they pulled out their headphones and put them on. On the walkway, Zero held up a hand, signaling. Redd's attention swept from her to Spike to the Toilet and back.

Ready. Waiting.

Zero dropped her hand in a cutting motion. An instant later the chains holding the Toilet released, a circumstance the creature didn't waste a moment to consider before throwing itself at a Cameraman, teeth bared. The Cameraman punched, knocking the Toilet backward. It recovered quickly though, snapping at Redd instead, who kicked it Spike's way. But the Speakerman was ready. He let loose a sonic cacophony that hit the Toilet like a bludgeon, stunning it instantly. It plummeted to the ground, and Redd sprang forward, deftly yanking on its flusher. The Toilet regained its senses just in time to be sucked away into nonexistence. Its bowl fell over, clanging against the metal floor, and was still.

Spike raised a hand for a high five, which Redd gladly obliged, though expeditiously. Zero was still watching, and she didn't put up with too much celebration when there was still work to be done. Still, when Redd looked to her, she gave him a satisfied thumbs-up. Meanwhile, a similar scene played out around the room. Blended teams of Cameramen and Speakermen, all learning to work together in order to best combine their skills against any Toilet-led threat. They'd been practicing these exercises for weeks, ever since the Speakermen had first shown up to save the day. Redd thought the training to make it into a squad had been intense, but the training for being *in* one was even more grueling, with the added component of actually going out and fighting the Toilets regularly. Though it had been strangely quiet since that day the unexpected excess of Skibidi Toilet forces had appeared. Redd wasn't a high enough rank to warrant knowing the theories why though, and Zero kept any info she might have had about it hidden away. Still, Redd had caught the gist of many conversations from a distance, and it was clear what the consensus was between the Cameramen and Speakermen leaders: The Toilets were up to something.

Spike seemed to understand that too but didn't care to pick the conclusion apart any further. He was relaxed in that way—serious enough when it came time for danger, but before then... Well, *we'll know what we need to know when we need to know it* seemed to be his take. Redd couldn't make himself adopt the same attitude. It was one thing to be good in a fight, but even the best soldier in the Alliance could be caught unawares if they weren't properly informed. What if there was some piece of intel that would be crucial to their squad surviving an encounter, and they didn't have it? He hadn't forgotten De4 and K5L. Not that being better informed would have saved them from the crushing weight of the Giant Toilet, which was the reason Redd also had an appreciation for the continued physical training.

Someone clapped him on the back: Spike. A low humming noise emanated from his speaker. He only made *that* noise when he thought Redd was caught up in overthinking something.

Redd shook his head. *I'm not.*

Spike shrugged. *"Relax,"* he buzzed.

The horn blared again: Zero, indicating for them to get ready for another drill. Redd moved into the next formation when suddenly one of the doors to the walkway above opened up and a Camerawoman came running in, gesturing vigorously to all the squad leaders to gather their teams and follow. Though she looked unsure of exactly why, Zero snapped her fingers at them. She wasn't as tough on the squad as she could be, but one thing Zero hated was to be kept waiting, so they all jumped to attention, leaving the training room behind and following their leader into one of the massive hangars. There they found what seemed like most of the base's population gathered, watching the large screen that was set into the far wall. There was a battle taking place, being transmitted live by one of the Cameramen present. Spike pumped a discreet fist enthusiastically. They'd seen plenty of big battles in playback as part of their training, but rarely while the fighting was still taking place.

Zero snapped her fingers again, pointing first at her lens and then the screen. *Pay attention. Watch what the enemy does. Figure out their weaknesses.*

Which would be easier to do with a better view. Redd spotted a crate nearby and climbed onto it, escaping the still growing sea of Cameramen and Speakermen. Spike, not about to be left behind, scrambled up beside him.

Strangely though, the battle didn't seem to be much of a learning experience. In fact, it was surprisingly tame as far as such things went. The Alliance forces seemed to have it under control, the Cameramen feeds switching every few minutes. One showed some of the Large Cameramen making short work of a handful of Toilets, flushing them without their smaller Speakermen counterparts needing to get involved. Another feed zoomed in on Alliance forces standing around, all the nearby enemy vanquished, or celebrating a job well done. There were a few Toilets either cornered or already captured; Redd wondered if their squad would be seeing them in the training room soon. But as the rotation of feeds continued, he became increasingly confused. There didn't seem to be much useful information coming in from this battle. Spike began to lose interest, instead pretending to be one of the Large Speakermen, towering over the others below, then acting like he was onstage, emitting a few bars of his favorite song, all drums and screeching guitars. Even Zero seemed perplexed, so much so that she didn't discipline Spike for slacking. Instead, she kept her attention on the screen, as if waiting for whatever it was they were *supposed* to be seeing to appear.

Which meant Redd was going to do that too.

A fresh feed showed Cameramen making their way down a city street, much like the previous ones. But this time, Redd recognized the area. It was the section of the city they'd been patrolling only a few weeks before, when they'd nearly been overrun by the Toilets. They hadn't been back since, but that didn't mean none of the Alliance forces had. As if to confirm this, a Large Cameraman suddenly appeared, coming around a corner. He was alone; if he'd been out with his squad, he must have gotten separated from them. Not surprising, it happened. But at least he'd been located. As Redd watched, a Camerawomen flagged him down and went running over.

The Large Cameraman remained where he was. Then his head twitched—once, twice. Before Redd could figure out why, the Large Cameraman lunged at the Camerawoman approaching him, grabbing her and lifting her like a child before ripping the head from her body.

A surprise screech sounded behind Redd. Spike was paying attention now. They *all* were.

On the screen, the broadcasting Cameraman turned to run. Or tried to.

A line of Toilets had appeared behind him and his group, grinning manically as their heads bobbed up and down, necks stretching disturbingly with excitement. Suddenly a bunch of tiny quick-moving Toilets appeared, threading through the spaces between the larger Toilets.

It was a trap. Redd realized that as the miniature scurrying Toilets closed in on their prey. Parasites, the Scientists had been calling them, tiny variants that could latch on to anyone and take command of their faculties, force them do things like tear their friends apart.

A sense of anger, tinged with visceral discomfort, spread through the hangar.

This was what they'd been gathered here to watch.

It was horrific. Redd felt sick as Spike's whole body slumped with disbelief. Nearby, Zero's fists were clenched so tightly that Redd was amazed she didn't tear holes in her gloves. She stared at the screen as the Cameraman was overrun, his feed cutting off to a blank, telling darkness. Another broadcast took its place, but Zero twisted away in rage, stalking to the very back of the room, where she looked angry enough to consider taking on the whole Skibidi Toilet army herself. Redd felt the same. Every time they thought the Toilets couldn't get more threatening, they trotted out some horrible new weapon like the parasites.

His attention was drawn back to the screen by the cheer that sounded when a squad being attacked stomped some of the diminutive assailants to death, as if they were no more than troublesome cockroaches. But that celebration was short-lived. More appeared almost instantly, overrunning the group, their feed cutting off abruptly as well.

It went on like that. More feeds, more parasites. For all the raging, bloody, explosion-riddle battles they'd seen, this simplistic overrunning of their forces by the enemy was somehow harder to endure. Not only were their comrades being taken over, but those infected by parasite control were also turning on their friends and allies. A hushed, grim silence fell over the room.

Still, as many of the onlookers began to drift away in shock, reaching their fill of the dreadful episodes, Redd kept watching. *Pay attention. Find their weaknesses.*

Oh, the parasites had vulnerabilities. They might be fast and agile, but they were still tiny compared to their targets. A well-placed foot or fist could take them out. But those were in short supply once a few members of a squad were turned. It was impossible for the Alliance teams to fight the enemy *and* themselves.

Up near the front of the hangar, a group of Cameramen Scientists remained as enraptured as Redd, pointing, taking notes, frantically gesturing among themselves. If there was a scientific way to undo what the parasites were doing, Redd was better off leaving them to find it. They were the smart ones. Instead, he focused on the parasites' movements, watching how they fared when jumping from high places, or from the ground, being sure to see where and what could offer them any sort of functional resistance. He wasn't going to fix the problem of possession by the Toilets, but he was certainly going to do his best to keep it from happening to anyone in his squad.

Suddenly something far worse than the Parasite Toilets appeared. Redd stiffened at the memory of De4 and K5L's last moments as they were thrown from the back of the Giant Toilet and slipped out of view to their deaths. This wasn't the Giant Toilet they'd fought against—that one was flushed away, like they all deserved to be—but it was even bigger and more monstrous, covered with green camouflage, with two massive laser cannons mounted on each side. Where the parasites attacked in a targeted fashion, this foe had a more bludgeoning, indiscriminate approach, loosing volley after volley of laser strikes at the fleeing Alliance forces. As they watched, a pair of Large Cameramen moved beneath the lasers' reach, trying to get close enough to scale the Giant Camo Toilet and reach its flusher. A handful of their smaller compatriots tried to help, including the Cameraman whose feed they were watching the events unfold on.

Right away, Redd saw the group wasn't going to make it. Had he and his squad looked as desperate as they leapt from the rooftop? No, desperate was the wrong word. He saw the determination in the Alliance forces, saw the plan the Large Cameramen had in mind. It was simply that it wasn't going to work. Before they could get close enough, smaller Toilets appeared in their way, blocking their advance long enough for the Camo Toilet to make short work of them with its unstoppable bulk. Then the lasers finished the job, firing a burst of vicious red energy that turned the feed to black.

It was silent in the hangar as another broadcast fed in.

This Cameraman had a more distant view, watching as the Camo Toilet continued its unstoppable march down a skyscraper-lined street, aided by Skibidi Toilets and infected Cameramen who ran alongside it like children following a parent. The Alliance was in retreat, but they had nowhere to go. That part of the city had become undisputed Toilet territory within minutes, though Redd wasn't sure why the enemy had bothered with it. It wasn't like there was much there to give them any special tactical or geographical advantage, at least as far as he could tell.

The Giant Camo Toilet reached an open area between buildings. Across from it, a block away, two Giant Speakermen stood their ground in the middle of the street, doing their best to cover the retreat of the Alliance members as reinforcements arrived to help. Redd wasn't sure even fresh troops would matter, not against this level of Toilet threat. Even the rocket launchers the Alliance had sent out failed to put a dent in its mottled carapace. Withdrawal seemed the only wise course of action as the Giant Camo Toilet's lasers kept up their relentless fire, giving the retreat a soundtrack of exploding concrete and breaking glass to accompany it.

And then . . . There was something else. A strange but not unfamiliar sound.

Spike jumped up suddenly, pumping a fist in the air as he let out an excited metallic wail. In the same moment that Redd recognized what he was hearing was music, a Titan Speakerman launched into view. The whole room erupted into applause. The Camo Toilet might be huge and seemingly unstoppable, but a *Titan* had arrived on the field of battle. They were the ultimate weapon of Alliance forces, unstoppable and without match, something the Titan Speakerman wasted no time in making clear. He squared off against the Giant Camo Toilet, undaunted by its weapons as he landed a wicked right hook, then stomped on a Large Toilet near its base. The Camo Toilet recovered, snapping at the Titan Speakerman, forcing him to withdraw a step. But only one. A moment later, the Titan attacked again, jumping into the air and kicking his foe across the face. Then, like it was nothing, the Titan Speakerman pulled its flusher.

The Camo Toilet was *done*.

But no one applauded. Something was wrong. Redd wasn't the only one who'd spotted the figures on the skyscraper behind the Titan Speakerman. And while it was hard to tell exactly what had happened from the distance they were seeing it at, a moment later the Titan Speakerman reached behind him, tearing a Parasite Toilet off his back. This one was far larger than the tiny variants they'd seen before . . . Almost as if it had been designed especially for the extra large Speakerman.

But as the Titan crushed the attacker, a cheer finally went up.

Redd didn't join in. *No!* He pointed, stabbing a finger at the screen as suddenly the Titan Speakerman went stiff and bent forward, a surge of electrical energy ripping through him. He turned away, shivering before going still and then standing straight once again. When the Titan Speakerman turned back so that he was facing the feed they were watching, Redd felt his knees go weak. This was no longer the Titan they knew as a friend and fierce ally. Immediately he turned and began firing on the Alliance forces without a moment's hesitation, sparing no one in his radius . . . As they all looked on, horrified, the Titan Speakerman raised his weapon again and fired.

The screen went black.

IT WASN'T CLEAR HOW MUCH TIME HAD PASSED when Spike finally tapped him on the shoulder, rousing Redd from the fugue he'd fallen into. He was still sitting on the crate, but the gathered Alliance forces had mostly dispersed from the hangar bay, trickling away in sad ones and twos, going back to . . . Redd didn't know. It seemed futile to go back to training after what they'd seen. Seemed futile to do, well . . . anything.

Spike waved at him. *"Okay?"*

The reverberating buzz of his voice was quiet, as if not wanting anyone to hear. Or maybe he was afraid to disrupt the stunned disbelief that still lingered in the hangar.

Redd shook his head. Okay was miles away from how he was. And Spike probably knew that too, probably wasn't in any better a mindset than Redd was. Worse even, Redd thought, realizing he was being selfish as Spike led him out of the hangar back into the halls of the base. Everyone they passed looked as if they'd gotten punched in the gut, but it was clearly worse for the Speakermen. The Titan

Speakermen were their heroes, their ultimate weapon, after all.

Redd paused in one of the halls near the Scientist laboratories, pointing at Spike. *What about you?*

Spike clenched and unclenched his fists at first. Then his shoulders dropped and he emitted a low, thrumming sound, tight with a sorrowful undercurrent.

Yeah. Redd nodded. He got it. How could they hope to win this war now, when one of their most powerful warriors was under the control of the enemy?

The worst part was they hadn't been able to do a single thing to stop what had happened. Only watched as it played out. The desire to go back in time and change it—to solve the problem instead of worry over it—coursed through Redd like electricity. But it was an energy he had nowhere to direct to. He kept moving instead, not paying attention to where he was going, not caring, only moving in order to have something to do besides replay that horrible moment the Parasite Toilet took control of their Titan ally. He was so lost in his thoughts that the only reason he stopped when passing one of the labs was the fact that he caught sight of Zero's distinctive jacket. It was a strange enough sight to arrest his progress—Zero wasn't a Scientist, wasn't handy with anything that wasn't a weapon—so why would she be hanging out in one of the labs?

He held up a hand to Spike. *Hold on a second.*

Redd leaned close to the door as he peered through the window, staying out of sight. Technically they weren't allowed in this area, but the figures inside seemed so engrossed with what they were doing that no one took notice of a Cameraman and Speakerman doing a touch of light spying. It wasn't only Zero there; all the squad leaders seemed to be gathered, along with Scientists and the other Alliance leaders of the base. The Lead Scientist, a Camerawoman with a crisp white jacket and weathered gray camera head, seemed to be demonstrating something, but they were too far away and the gathered figures too clumped up for Redd to see what was going on. Slowly he pressed his fingers to the door and pushed it open, praying it wouldn't squeak.

Spike startled, waving a hand apprehensively. *What are you doing?*

Redd pointed into the room. *I want to know what's going on.*

Spike dropped his hands, head lolling back in exasperation, but when Redd crept in, he followed, keeping close. They made their way over to a control console, crouching down behind it. The vantage was much better here, and Redd could now see the group was gathered around a handheld screen. It was replaying recordings of the Parasite Toilets infecting Alliance forces, including the Titan Speakerman. The videos kept zooming in, and when they did, the nearby Scientists would start scribbling notes furiously on their clipboards.

Spike shifted uncomfortably and shrugged when Redd looked his way. *Why are we bothering with this?*

But Redd held up a finger. *Just a little longer.*

He turned back, creeping a little farther along the console, one hand holding its edge to steady him. It brushed against something. Redd felt it just in time to see a pencil roll over the edge of the console. It hit the floor with a faint clink.

Redd winced, sensing Spike do the same behind him. But the noise was quiet; no one seemed to notice.

Well, not *no one*. Arms crossed, Zero stood at the back of the pack. And she didn't miss anything. At the errant sound, her head spun their way, spotting them behind their makeshift hiding spot. She tightened, looking back at the others, but they were still engrossed with the videos. Redd could tell she was *not* happy when her lens swung back their way.

She waved one hand impatiently. *What are you doing? Get out of here!*

Redd was about to obey—he would never ignore a direct order from his squad leader—when the video on the screen changed once again. The recordings were gone. Instead, an animation began to play, also drawing Zero's attention, showing the rough outlines of the larger Parasite Toilets that had taken over the Titan Speakerman. They quickly shrank down, turning into the more common smaller parasites, shown in comparison to an average-sized Cameraman. On the screen, the animated parasite leapt onto the back of the Cameraman's neck, infecting him. The Lead Scientist pointed to this as the animation continued to rotate around the newly attached creature, highlighting what pieces of information the Alliance seemed to know about them, which were notably few.

Then the screen switched again to show, from a safe distance, a gathering of Skibidi Toilets marching through a street, half a dozen enthralled Speakermen and Cameramen among their ranks. *That.* The Lead Scientist indicated the controlled figures. *We need test subjects to examine. We need to go out there and capture the infected.*

Zero's hand shot into the air immediately. *Here!* She waved at the Lead Scientist. *I volunteer my squad.*

The Lead Scientist nodded and gave her a thumbs-up. *You got it.*

Zero held her head high, waiting for the others' attention to go back to the briefing before subtly turning her lens toward Redd and Spike again. *You ready to do this?*

Redd gave her a thumbs-up too. He was. In fact, he was more excited than he could express to be given a chance to *do* something. Dangerous or not, they had to try something to stop this parasitic toilet infection before it took down any more of the Alliance.

THERE WAS NO TIME TO WASTE. ZERO HAD THE squad reoutfitted and back on the city streets the next day. They weren't about to be caught unarmed; Zero and a higher-ranking Speakerman who'd temporarily joined them carried laser guns, and the rest of the squad shock sticks, handheld batons whose tip sent an intense electric shock through whatever they touched. But this was no normal patrol. Instead of street-by-street sweeps, they kept to the alleys and shadows as much as they could, creeping their way through the city, always ready for an unexpected encounter. They passed through the area where the Titan Speakerman had been infected; it was strange, to be where it had happened. What had been the location of a fierce battle was now as quiet as a grave. Which was an apt description; bodies of fallen allies still littered the area, not yet safe enough to risk sending in clean-up crews. But it was exactly because it *wasn't* safe that their squad was there. Live feeds were few and far between in this section of the city right now, but enough infected Alliance members had been spotted nearby that this had been designated as their hunting grounds.

In addition to the new weapons, Spike and a Camerawoman also carried net-firing launchers. The idea was to corner a small group of the enemy, take out the Toilets, and capture the infected. It sounded straightforward enough. But even though he was still a new recruit, Redd knew there were a million things that could go wrong.

They made their way along the deserted streets,

into an area where everything seemed to grow tighter, the buildings dense and pressed up against each other like bricks in a wall. Hardly any sunlight reached here, casting most of the area in dim shadows, and leaving a lot of alleys dark enough to hide anything that might lurk within them. Debris and trash littered the asphalt—battles must have raged here recently—but Redd was thankful for the destruction as they passed a building with a glassy, reflective exterior that had mostly been smashed at street level. They had to carefully pick through the shards of broken glass to remain quiet, but at least they didn't risk a reflection giving them away to some enemy hidden just out of sight.

Zero held up a hand and clenched it into a fist. *Hold up.*

The squad obeyed, readying their weapons in case an attack was imminent. But while nothing appeared, as they waited, Redd became aware of faint sounds nearby—voices, speaking an unmistakable language. Zero shook her fist quickly, confirming what he already knew. There were Skibidi Toilets nearby. Unlike their usual orders, which were to kill every Toilet they encountered, they had new, very specific guidelines about engagement: If there were no infected with the Toilets to try and capture, and the Toilets didn't spot them, the squad was to move on so as not to risk creating unnecessary commotion and being discovered. Redd was certain that part of the orders rubbed Zero the wrong way. After all, it went against her nature to leave Toilets alive and well, unless there was no other choice.

Their squad leader guided them forward again, moving closer to the buildings until they were inching along the concrete edge of the closest, heading toward a blind corner. When Zero reached it, she risked a quick look around, snapping back an instant later. She turned to the squad and nodded.

Toilets. She held up a hand with three fingers raised. *Three infected.*

Perfect. Redd clenched his shock stick tighter. They were going for it.

With a series of quick gestures, Zero silently laid out their plan, then raised three fingers again. This time, it was a countdown.

Three . . .

Beside him, Spike readied, even though he'd be moving in last, hoping to get a good shot at one of the infected while they and the Toilets were busy with the rest of the squad.

Two . . .

Something glinted on a ledge above Spike. Something small with a white bowl. Redd shoved Spike out of the way just as the Parasite Toilet leapt, stabbing with his shock stick as he pushed; it connected with the parasite, electricity surging throughout the creature and exploding it with a satisfying pop.

A *loud* pop.

Redd turned in time to catch Zero's shock and the squad's surprise. But there was no chance to get scolded; a screech of alarm came from ahead of them. More Toilet parasites appeared on the ledges, and the group of enemies the squad had been stalking suddenly poured around the corner of the building. Zero didn't signal for retreat. She—like all of them—realized there was no avoiding a conflict, not now. There was only fighting back and maybe completing their mission, or else ending up dead.

Zero raised her weapon and fired at the nearest approaching Toilet as two of its parasite counterparts jumped at Redd. He dodged the first but was barely fast enough to swing his shock stick like a club at the other. Still, he managed a glancing blow that sent it flying into the concrete wall, where it slid to the ground, stunned. A foot came down on the one he'd dodged; it was Spike's. The Speakerman let out a sound of alarm and pointed as more of the parasites began to rain down. Redd backed away from the wall to get out of their leaping range, swinging over and over at the tiny Toilet swarm. Meanwhile, the Speakerman with the laser gun picked a few off in mid-flight as the rest of the squad smashed the ones that managed to land on the street. But the parasites weren't their only concern. An infected Speakerman grabbed one of the squad Cameramen, arms wrapping around him in a bear hug. The parasites were ready; one skittered up onto the restrained Cameraman's shoulders, latching on immediately. Nearby, a trio of regular Toilets surrounded the Speakerman with the laser; he shot one of them, but the other two attacked, pushing him down to the asphalt. Redd watched as the Speakerman's hands went limp, releasing the weapon. Redd darted forward, grabbing the gun while the pair were still occupied with their prey and fired on them. The Toilets screeched and fell away dead, but it was too late for the Speakerman.

This was bad. Redd could see it. And he was pretty sure Zero could see it too. There seemed to be dozens of the Parasite Toilets, gathered almost as if they were expecting plenty of potential Alliance victims. Or maybe the squad had simply been unlucky in the enemy they'd come across. Either way, one thing was clear: They weren't going to win this fight. The pained frustration in Zero's stance was clear as she shot two more Toilets, then began signaling the squad to retreat. Most obeyed, but Spike had his back to her and missed the gesture. Redd ran to him, electrocuting another Parasite Toilet intent on capturing his friend. Then he spun Spike around and indicated their fleeing comrades.

Go!

Spike looked unsure, looking from Redd to Zero and back, but as Redd hefted the laser gun, he understood. Redd would take up the rear with their leader, make sure everyone got away. Spike bolted off as Redd fell in beside Zero. They fired in unison—one high, one low—targeting the Toilets closest to them. Zero, a crack shot, picked them off easily. Redd wasn't quite as good, but he managed to keep the enemy at bay. The infected Cameraman from their squad was down too; Redd wasn't sure if that was his work or Zero's. Wasn't sure he wanted to know.

A hand slapped his upper arm: Zero's, indicating it was time to go. She turned and ran. Redd followed, but as he did, a flash of white glinted in the corner of his vision. He ducked . . . but not fast enough. A Parasite Toilet alighted on his shoulder. Redd slapped at it, blows which it dodged, though it seemed to move slower than the others. Then before he could stop it, the parasite skittered around to the base of Redd's neck. A caustic spike of pain surged through him, his back arching so much that he was suddenly looking up at the sky, and then . . .

Nothing.

STATIC.

His vision crackled with it—bursts of gray, pale flickers of green . . .

The world shocked into view, suddenly clear. No, not entirely; there was a strange, vaguely muted look to everything, as if Redd had smeared a thin coating of gray grease on his lens. Colors seemed washed out and the edges of his vision blurred with darkness.

He was standing in the middle of the road, a Toilet coming right at him. Redd tried to take a step back, clenched his fist and was ready to . . .

None of that happened. He didn't move an inch. And the Toilet passed right by him, as if he didn't exist. Suddenly Redd turned and *followed* the Toilet. It wasn't alone. There were at least a dozen enemies surrounding him, ordinary grunts and a pair of spindly Striders too. None seemed to take any notice of Redd. He tried to stop, to fall back from the enemy group—or better, attack them—but no matter what he did, his limbs refused to obey. One foot in front of the other, he trailed the Toilets dutifully, like a baby duckling with its mother.

They'd gone several blocks until he finally understood what was happening.

Another Cameraman joined them, and a Speakerwoman. They merged with the group, taking places right in front of Redd. On each, a Parasite Toilet was planted squarely on the nape of their necks. They were infected.

Which meant . . . so was he.

No! He couldn't be—they'd taken out all the parasites that were close enough to reach them . . . hadn't they? In the confusion of the fight, Redd couldn't be sure. The last thing he'd seen was Zero, fleeing after the rest of the squad. Had they all gotten away? Were they all safe? The questions ached within him, impossible to answer. Wherever Redd was now, he didn't recognize it; the shock of the parasite's takeover must have scrambled him for a while. Hours . . . maybe even days . . .

Static flickered in his vision again. Suddenly the street was gone. Instead, they were in an enclosed hallway, no place he'd been before but not entirely unfamiliar. The walls were gray and reinforced-looking, broken occasionally by thick metal doors controlled by touch screen panels. They passed a corridor—down which Redd caught a glimpse of an assembly line, covered in half-finished lasers like the ones he'd seen mounted on some Toilets—and then a line of windows looking into a lab, where experiments he couldn't begin to recognize were taking place. From all this, plus the plethora of Toilets, Redd surmised they must be in a base.

A Skibidi Toilet base.

Frustration burned within him like a furnace. He didn't know what was worse—being under enemy control, or having a hundred Toilets within reach but unable to do the one thing he wanted to do: smash each and every one of their ugly faces into something that wouldn't be recognizable as human, alien, or anything else.

Though he couldn't turn his head, there were more infected Cameramen and Speakermen in front of them. It seemed that they were all being escorted somewhere; their Toilet chaperones led them into a large room, empty save for more infected. And from the way the door clamped shut and locked immediately, it was clear they were being kept prisoner when not being used to fight. Redd stopped in a corner, looking out at the others in this cell. They looked barely awake, their heads slumped slightly forward, arms hanging slack at their sides. It was hard to tell exactly what was up with them though, when he couldn't move to get a better . . .

He was in the city again.

Laser guns fired, blasts clipping the buildings above him, sending bits of concrete and stone raining down. He was running toward an oncoming wave of Alliance forces—Cameramen and Speakermen ground troops, followed by heavy armored vehicles mounted with laser cannons. One turned its barrel in Redd's direction and fired. The Toilet parasite piloting him dodged the blast at the last second, then dodged the fists of a ten-foot-tall Large Speakerman. A Cameraman wielding a baseball bat came next; the parasite danced Redd back out of range as he swung.

Then Redd's fist was balled, smashing the ally-turned-enemy's face. Glass shards flew as the Cameraman went down and Redd jumped on top of him, punching over and over again until . . .

He tried to shut off his sight, to not see what was happening, but the evil, seemingly endless attack wouldn't go away. Finally the parasite set them hunting for a new target, settling on a nearby Speakerwoman who was preparing to sonic blast a cluster of incoming Toilets. Redd grabbed her right before she let loose, hands closing on her speaker and wrenching it around. There was a terrible metal-scraping-against-metal sound, and she went limp, crumpling into a heap at his feet.

They kept moving.

No. He didn't want to do this. With every attack, with every fallen comrade, Redd felt as if he was the one being broken, torn apart, and smashed into a pulp. This wasn't him. This was the parasite, controlling him like a puppet, forcing him to do awful acts he would never engage in otherwise. Still, it *was* him, was his body, punching holes through the Alliance lines, clearing the way for the grunt Toilets. As he watched, helpless to stop it, a Toilet clambered onto an armored vehicle and ripped its driver from the seat, throwing him to the Strider Toilets below, who waited like a pack of wild dogs hoping to be fed. Following that, the parasite directed him onto the vehicle as well, pointing him toward the mounted laser and its Cameraman operator. The Cameraman stood his ground, landing a pair of brutal punches that rattled Redd. He might not be able to control his body, but he could still feel the pain inflicted on it. Another punch put Redd on his back, quickly followed by a kick to his middle that crunched agonizingly.

Good. Redd was staring into the face of the Cameraman attacking him, hoping that he could see the desperation that lay behind Redd's lens. *Take me out,* he tried to communicate silently. That was the best option for the Alliance now . . . and for him. *Stop me from hurting any more of our friends.*

Instead, as the foot came down again, Redd's hand grabbed it and yanked, sending the Cameraman tumbling off the vehicle. In an instant, Redd was upright again and going for the laser. He took the controls, swinging the weapon around so that it was pointed at the Cameraman on the ground. Still stunned, the Cameraman was barely able to push himself up off the asphalt with one arm and raise the other in self-defense. But the gesture was useless. The laser would cut through him like a hot knife through butter, and Redd's fingers were already tightening around the trigger.

NO!

His hands froze. Only for an instant, but it was enough time for the Cameraman to regain clarity. A second later, Redd squeezed the trigger. But the laser found only the space where the Cameraman had been an instant before, leaving a dark scorch mark across the pavement. The parasite forced him to swing the weapon around again, to take aim at the back of his fleeing ally, but by then a Large Cameraman had come up beside the vehicle. One hand grabbed the end of the laser and forced it toward the street. The other reached for Redd.

The parasite was having none of that. Redd abandoned the controls before jumping to the street and bolting, his alien puppeteer apparently deciding the threat was larger than it wanted to deal with. They joined the Skibidi Toilet troops, regathering as the Alliance forces rallied and pushed them back. As a retreat began, Redd replayed the moment at the laser controls over and over again. It had been so brief, barely a heartbeat's worth of time, but for a moment it seemed that he'd . . . hesitated? That he'd regained control of himself just long enough to give the Cameraman a chance. But no, it must have been some sort of glitch. Or the parasite had been momentarily distracted. No matter how he tried, Redd had no control—not of his legs, hands, camera, *nothing*. Not an inch of him would obey. All he could do was watch as he continued to be a pawn fighting on the wrong side of this pitiless war.

BACK IN THE CELL. ANOTHER BATTLE. BACK IN THE cell. Like a bad dream, it played out over and over until Redd's anger burned away, leaving only despair. He'd lost count of how many Alliance members he'd taken down, but the memories of them haunted him as they moved him from one part of the city to another, one fight to the next. Some of the other infected fell; more were captured to fill their places.

And then he saw the infected Titan Speakerman again. It was the worst battle so far, a massive engagement that took place at the edge of the sprawling metro, where there were fewer skyscrapers to hamper the Titan's movement. Unfortunately there was also an Alliance outpost hidden among the warehouses there. Redd wondered how the Toilets knew about it. Could the parasites glean intel from their victims? He couldn't tell. The Toilets talked among themselves, but in their strange, jumpy language, of which he could catch only the odd word or two. More likely, they had spies everywhere, trying to flush out Alliance nests, infiltrate their bases. Redd hoped that his squad was safe in their base and that it was still secret; unfortunately hope was as much assistance as he had to give right now.

For the outpost, he couldn't even offer that. The Toilet forces swept through it, destroying everything—and everyone—they came across. All with the help of the Titan Speakerman, who ripped a whole wall off the warehouse that housed the outpost, like it was the foil wrapper off a piece of candy. Remove wall, fire a couple volleys in, and then—that's all, folks. The Toilets infiltrated and exterminated. Redd watched his hands beat a Scientist Cameraman into unconsciousness, then use a machete taken from a fallen Speakerman to hack the lower legs off a Camerawoman. She floundered, unable to run. Redd's parasite merely piloted him further into the fray, leaving her to be finished off by the Toilet grunts that would come after.

When the bulk of the fighting was over, the Titan Speakerman blasted off—headed, no doubt, to whatever battle the Toilets needed him at next. Acidic frustration suddenly surged through Redd again. He'd thought his fury was spent, but seeing the Titan being controlled in the same manner he was . . . It was unconscionable, unfair, and unbelievable that the Toilets could use a *Titan* like that, much less anyone else.

And yet, simmering in his anger was all he could do until a sound caught his and the parasite's attention. It came from a nearby closet. Redd ripped the door open to find a Scientist Cameraman cowering within. He clutched some sort of tangle of circuit boards and wires in a metal framework, an invention perhaps. The Scientists were always trying to develop something that would give the Alliance an advantage in the war. But whatever this was, it wouldn't be what turned the tide. Redd's hand grabbed the contraption and Redd's foot smashed it into a million unrecognizable pieces. The Scientist watched in horror, hands up, shaking with fear, anger, and probably a dozen other emotions. Then suddenly his shoulders dropped. As Redd closed in, the Scientist did nothing, simply stared miserably at the floor, awaiting his fate. The parasite forced Redd to raise the machete, readying to bring it down on the hopeless Scientist . . .

Suddenly his hand snapped open. The blade fell, clanging against the metal floor.

Redd didn't move. He didn't *want* to move, and he hadn't wanted to bring the blade down either.

And surprisingly he'd done neither.

The Scientist stared quizzically, as if trying to figure out what happened. Then—because Scientists were smart, after all—he thought better of that and pushed past Redd, escaping into the half-destroyed outpost.

Redd's arm dropped. Not of his own volition—that movement definitely belonged to the parasite—but the other movement, stopping the attack on the Scientist . . . He *had* done that. The laser cannon hadn't been a fluke.

Somehow, he was taking control again.

IT WAS HIT OR MISS. SOMETIMES REDD WAS ABLE to take control, hold it for a few precious seconds before the parasite's will overrode his again. He managed it most often during the battles, though it still wasn't enough control to either stop the horrors he was inflicting or direct himself into a situation he wouldn't walk away from. But he was careful. He'd learned quick. One of the first times he'd managed to take over, when he'd stopped himself from grabbing a fleeing Speakerwoman as she passed too close, a grunt Toilet had looked at him askance. Just for a moment before it continued along its path of destruction, but that was enough to make Redd act more cautiously during subsequent attempts to regain his body.

He made progress back in the cell as well, managing to stay awake a little longer each time he returned. In those moments, he tried to figure out what was allowing him to do this. None of the other infected, including those that had been under Toilet control nearly as long has he had, seemed to be able to do what he did. No, they all seemed 100 percent puppet, fodder to fight or be sacrificed as needed. But something must be different with him. Maybe some quirk of his training? A particular piece of hardware that he had and the others didn't?

Then, in a burst of clarity, he figured it out. It came to him as he swung a metal pipe at a Speakerman, stopping him from letting loose a sonic attack by smashing part of his speaker. The day he'd been infected, he'd hit one of the Parasite Toilets in a similar way, hadn't he? Clipped one, sending it careening into the nearby wall, where it had fallen. Then he'd lost track of it. The parasite definitely hadn't been destroyed, but maybe . . . Maybe it had been damaged? That was it, he realized. The parasite must have been injured somehow, in a way that was so minor that none of the other Toilets, including the parasite itself, had realized it. But also in a way that was crucial enough that as time went on, its control over Redd was beginning to falter. To glitch.

Not fast enough for him, but it *was* happening.

THE SKIBIDI TOILET BASE WAS A TENSE PIT OF frustration as they returned from another conflict. Despite what Redd was forced to do, the Alliance had definitively won this one, leaving the Toilets angry and snapping at each other, but leaving Redd glad for it. Although he wasn't as lucky as some of the other infected—rather than being rescued by the Alliance, he'd simply returned to the Toilet base. Not unscathed though, not this time. A massive gash ran down one arm, where a Speakerman's reluctant knife swing had caught him. The wound sparked and sent electric pulses of pain through him; still, he seemed to have full use of his hand and fingers.

But instead of returning to his usual cell, Redd's parasite piloted him deeper into the Skibidi Toilet base, to a section Redd hadn't seen yet. It was several levels down from the prisoners' cells in an area that seemed to have far fewer doors than the floors above, and each door had more locks. One door slid open as they passed, allowing a Researcher Toilet to exit; Redd caught a brief glimpse of the room beyond. The face that he saw there sent a spike of fear through him. Any member of the Alliance would know those needle-sharp eyes and gray-haired visage: Chief Scientist Skibidi Toilet. He was hard at work, his pronged metal appendages moving with rapid purpose across the exposed electronics of . . .

No. It couldn't be.

The door slid shut, cutting off Redd's view, but he knew what he'd seen: G-Toilet himself.

It was surreal seeing the leader of the Skibidi Toilets in the flesh, even for an instant. Redd itched to turn around, to further observe whatever it was the Chief Scientist was doing to the invaders' leader . . .

But what did it matter? It wasn't as if Redd could tell anyone what he saw.

The parasite kept them moving deeper into the facility until they arrived in a large round laboratory. Examination tables were set up throughout it, some empty, others sporting damaged Toilets or infected Alliance members. The Toilets that puttered their way from tables to control panels and back were clearly of a more advanced version, like the Alliance Scientists back at Redd's base. Some were engaged in repairing the Toilets damaged in battle; others seemed to be acting out more nefarious tasks. A heavily damaged infected Speakerman lay sprawled out on a table. *Formerly* infected, that was. His parasite sat off to one side of the surface, watching enthusiastically as the Researcher Toilets sawed into the Speakerman's head, poking the interior with tools and instruments Redd didn't recognize.

Fresh anger rushed through him. Watching the

Speakerman be violated in such a way was revolting, even if he was lucky enough to be dead already. But clearly that's what the infected were to the Toilets—disposable weapons to be used in battle or, if they became too damaged, lab rats to be dissected or experimented on. And whatever they were doing must be important if Chief Scientist Toilet *and* G-Toilet could be found here. If only the Alliance could see this place and the horrors it contained . . . If only they could figure out where it was and plan a strike to infiltrate and destroy it . . .

So intense was his desire to share what he was witnessing that, for a moment, Redd didn't realize he was broadcasting. It was only for a few seconds, his feed going live and dead again almost as soon as he realized it was happening. But for that precious stretch of time, what he was witnessing could have been seen by *anyone* in the Alliance, as long as they were tuned in to his signal. Cold fear spread like frost. Had the Toilets noticed what he'd done? Had the parasite controlling him realized it? It had seemingly remained unaware of the other slivered moments of control, but this was different. Surely sending out a live feed was something the parasite wouldn't be able to ignore or write off as a glitch.

A trio of Researcher Toilets suddenly turned toward Redd.

This was it. They'd noticed. A strange sense of relief mixed with his apprehension. If he'd become a liability, they would surely get rid of him. He pushed aside what would come after, when he'd be picked apart like the Speakerman nearby, focusing only on the fact that finally, *thankfully*, he'd never have to fight another one of his comrades again. Never have to watch them go limp and lifeless because of what his hands had done.

The Toilets herded him backward until he was pushed up against one of the exam surfaces. Then the parasite guided him onto it so that he was sitting upright. Redd held his resolve tighter as the Researcher Toilets converged, their gruesome tools raised. This was right—this was what *should* happen after everything he'd done. He waited for the darkness to come, to free in him a way he'd never be as long as the parasite was attached.

But he was disappointed again. As much as Redd welcomed the end, the Toilets weren't done with him yet. They went to work on his arm, repairing the damage there with a series of rapid, efficient procedures. Redd couldn't even hang his head in defeat, only continued to look where the parasite pointed his lens—out at the sick goings-on before him.

Or . . . Maybe he *could* do something. Even if he got caught, it would be worth it: broadcasting whatever few minutes of intel he could before the Toilets realized what was happening, and hope that someone in the Alliance would pick it up.

Why not try? What did he have to lose at this point? *Nothing.* That's what.

Redd concentrated, ignoring the strange sensations as the Toilets tinkered with his wound, intent only on the act of broadcasting. Nothing happened at first—he wasn't sure how he'd managed it the first time—but he didn't give up. Didn't care about what happened if he got caught. A few more moments of intense effort passed, then . . .

Yes! He was doing it, his feed broadcasting out into the world. He focused on holding it as the parasite kept him staring forward, watching the fallen Alliance infected being experimented on. Another damaged infected Cameraman was dragged in as Redd watched, brought over to one of the empty tables directly across from him. Immediately it was clear that the Cameraman was a goner; he was tattered and torn, one leg missing and an arm damaged so badly it could hardly be called that anymore. The Researcher Toilets made the same call. They turned away, not bothering with any attempted fixes. Except for one—the executioner, Redd assumed. The one that would put the Cameraman down fully so they could start their sick experiments on his remains.

Instead, it moved around to the head of the table. The Cameraman had been laid on its side, leaving the parasite infecting it exposed. The Researcher Toilet leaned in close to it and muttered a few low words, then laughed. Redd's arm twitched with rage from the cruel sound of it, nearly breaking his concentration and sending a bolt of fear through him. Fortunately the Toilets repairing the limb seemed to chalk it up to an involuntary movement. Forcing himself to relax, he refocused on broadcasting. The Researcher Toilet across the room was saying something else to the parasite. Suddenly the parasite unlatched itself. The Cameraman shot up in a panic, limbs flailing despite his injuries as he looked around with wild confusion. Then he tried to run. One leg down, he fell immediately yet still tried to crawl for the door, either unwilling to give up or in such a bewildered frenzy that he didn't realize the futility of his situation. Around him, the Researcher Toilets paused in their work to laugh at the injured Cameraman as he inched pitifully along.

Don't react. Keep the feed live. So much anger welled up in Redd that it was a miracle that he could remain still, keep broadcasting. But this was more than useful intel—what he was witnessing was seismic in its revelation. The infected had been assumed to be lost causes so far—once taken by the Toilets, there was no saving them. But he was witnessing something that contradicted that. If the parasites were removed, then the target they'd infected regained control of themselves.

Please, Redd pleaded silently. Someone be watching.

Pain shot through him again as the Researcher Toilets working on him hit something vital in his arm. Redd stopped broadcasting, afraid to push his luck. His timing was spot on; that seemed to be the last of the repair. The Toilets used a tiny laser to seal him back up again, leaving nothing worse than a torn coat sleeve. Then they backed away, blubbering something in their Skibidi language to the parasite. Redd was forced to stand up, good as new again and ready to be thrown back into the next fight.

Across the room, the Toilets grew bored with watching the escape attempt. One of the grunt Toilets jumped at an order from a Researcher to deal with the situation. It was over quickly. So quickly that Redd found he envied the now-still Cameraman, even as they dragged the body back onto the table to begin dissecting.

It was tempting to make the same escape attempt, but Redd couldn't do it. Not now. Not if he could continue his broadcasts, share out every moment possible to the Alliance in the hope they'd receive the intel that would help them save the infected, maybe even shift the balance of the war. For all the damage he'd done against his allies and friends, this was the price he had to pay. The thing that might make everything that had happened worth it.

Don't worry, he assured himself. Sooner or later, the Toilets would figure out that his parasite was malfunctioning. Then he'd be free of this.

Then it would be over.

EVERY CHANCE HE GOT, REDD BROADCASTED. WHEN he was moving through the base, when the Toilets babbled at each other, when they dragged him into a battle (especially when it seemed like an ambush). Never more than a short feed; he was still cognizant that the Toilets might get wise any moment, and though he'd accepted that inevitability, he wanted to make sure he got out the maximum amount of intel before it happened.

So when a massive gathering of Toilets occurred in one of the larger chambers of the base, he began to transmit. The infected were stationed in the very back of the space like toys waiting to be played with, but it was clear something big was happening. This was more Toilets than Redd had ever seen gathered in a single location—countless grunts, Striders, Helicopter Toilets buzzing around their heads like giant insects and, horribly, a small army of tiny parasites bubbling with excitement over the chance to infect an Alliance member. No Chief Scientist Toilet or G-Toilet, unfortunately, but he knew better than to expect this was their sole base of operation.

Careful not to move too intentionally, Redd managed to stand a little straighter, get a better angle of the front of the space, where the Toilets in charge were conferring with one another. To him, it almost seemed like they were arguing—no, they appeared . . .

concerned? But there was no time to figure out what was vexing them. The Toilet in charge, clad in a battle-scarred green helmet, turned to the gathering and barked some unintelligible order; shortly after, they were marching into the city. There they were joined by half a dozen Giant Toilets, two covered in camouflage markings with mounted lasers and one with vicious buzz saw attachments that screeched with anticipation of the coming fight.

Redd heard the battle long before he saw it, explosions and the heated sound of laser fire growing closer and closer. He stumbled as a missile landed so close that the asphalt beneath him heaved, the parasite catching their balance at the last moment. If only the explosion had been a little closer. It wasn't the first time in a fight Redd had wished for a quick end so he wouldn't do what he was about to do, but he steeled himself and risked a few seconds of a broadcast. It was clear that they were arriving as reinforcements; whatever they were headed into, the Skibidi Toilets must be losing. If so, maybe his broadcast would give the Alliance some warning that more of the enemy was coming. Luckily the Titan Speakerman was nowhere to be seen, though if he'd been nearby, Redd supposed they wouldn't have been called up to help in the first place.

Then suddenly they were in the thick of it. Alliance forces were everywhere, positioned around a plaza scattered with the remains of destroyed fountains and sculptures, coming at the newly arrived Toilet force from all angles. Projectiles flew through the smoke-filled air as another explosion took out a brick building less than a block away, though Redd didn't see which side inflicted the damage. Strider Toilets skittered across the remains of a once-colorful mural as Alliance drones dipped through the air, trying to avoid Helicopter Toilets while, below that, a group of Large Speakermen attempted to scale a Giant Toilet to reach its flusher.

It was pure chaos, no matter what direction the parasite turned him in.

Again and again, Redd sent out short bursts of his visual feed, until there was so much smoke and debris surrounding him that there wasn't any point. He could barely see the fights he was being steered into, much less anything else. He punched a Camerawoman, then dodged the knives of a Speakerman. Another Speakerwoman appeared only steps away, readying a sonic attack. Redd wouldn't have had time to stop her, but to his disappointment, a pair of Skibidi Toilets knocked her to the ground. Thankfully more Alliance members came to her rescue, flushing the Toilets and dragging her to safety.

A Large Cameraman appeared and grabbed at Redd. His massive arms swept across Redd's vision as he dodged, jumping backward, though the remains of a wall behind him hampered his escape. Redd's attacker lunged again, but damaged or not, the parasite managed to keep them just out of reach. *Stop trying to fight me by hand,* Redd wanted to communicate, *and find a weapon. Get this over with!* But it was clear the Large Cameraman had other intentions. Finally Redd caught on. He'd had the same assignment once, hadn't he? No doubt the Alliance was still trying to capture the infected in order to find some way to fix them.

Just get rid of the parasite! Redd tried to take control and point at his neck, but before he could manage it, there was another detonation. Not as close as the last, but debris began raining down on them. A chunk of concrete the size of a watermelon hit the Large Cameraman in the head; he fell to one knee. Redd was pummeled too, the force of the pieces colliding with him enough to spin him like a toy top. In the smoke and confusion, he lost the Large Cameraman, as well as all sense of direction of where he'd been and which way he'd been going.

A humanoid shape appeared in the haze. With a quickness that felt almost desperate, Redd's parasite threw him at it. He collided with the figure, knocking it to the ground, then began throwing brutal punches before it was even clear that his foe was a Speakerman. No, not just any Speakerman . . .

Spike! Cold recognition flooded Redd as his fists fell again and again on his friend, who was trying to fight him off, to no avail.

Use your sonic attack! Spike was being battered, but it made no sense. He was tougher than this; Redd had seen that on plenty of occasions. One blast from his speaker would easily throw Redd off, stun him long enough for his friend to do what Redd hoped he was willing to do. But Spike wasn't even fighting back; he was only holding his arms up defensively. He didn't *want* to fight back, Redd realized, didn't want to harm his friend any more than Redd wanted to harm him. But the Parasite Toilet didn't care; it would kill them both without a second thought.

Well, if Spike wasn't going to do anything, Redd

would have to. As his fist descended once more toward his friend, he took control, stopping the arm in mid-swing, though it took every ounce of his concentration to do so. Below him, Spike let his guard drop. For a moment, they were frozen like that, the battle storming around them.

Run! Redd thought desperately, hoping his friend would get the message. *I can't hold it forever!*

Whatever Spike understood, it was enough. He shoved Redd off himself and rolled away, getting back on his feet. Unfortunately Redd followed suit, under parasite control again as his strength faltered. He fought to regain autonomy and managed to briefly shake his head at Spike. *No! Don't sacrifice yourself trying to help me! Do what needs to be done!*

But Spike didn't attack. He simply stood where he was, fists raised, waiting.

Idiot! Redd managed to stop his foot from taking a step forward, straining against the parasite. It was getting harder and harder, but he couldn't allow himself to attack Spike again. Couldn't bear being the death of his friend like he had been for so many other members of the Alliance. *Stop me!*

But Spike only looked around, as if waiting for something. The smoke was beginning to clear a little, and more Alliance forces appeared. Redd felt something twist inside him as several members of his squad appeared, weaving through the piles of rubble, forming a half circle around him. But none prepared to strike, or engage him in any way.

What are you waiting for? Redd tried to beckon them on, to show them it was okay, but they didn't make a move. The parasite did though, backing him away as it seemed to grasp that, friends or not, they wouldn't remain passive forever. Suddenly Redd's foot hit something. The parasite paused their retreat and they looked down. Instead of a piece of debris, as Redd had expected, something far worse waited below. A laser rifle, dropped by some fallen Alliance member.

No! Redd tried to stop the parasite as it forced him to grab the weapon. It was no use; he barely managed to slow the raising of it, feeling sick as his finger slipped behind the trigger and his other hand pointed the barrel toward his squad.

Toward Spike.

Finally his friend looked ready to run. But despite every last ounce of Redd's willpower being thrown at stopping the parasite's movements, it was already too late.

Another figure came into view suddenly, appearing over a mountain of debris like a rising sun.

Zero! She was armed with a weapon that Redd didn't recognize, a strange, glowing rifle that was pointed directly at him.

Finally. A sense of calm came over Redd as Zero fired. The blast hit him square in the chest, as hard and heavy as a perfectly landed punch. But it didn't hurt. Instead, a chilly, buzzing energy coursed through Redd, reaching from the tips of his fingers down to his toes, but gathering most assertively at the nape of his neck. The Parasite's screech seemed to come from within his head, but it was a welcome sound. Redd was suddenly filled with a new sensation, one he never thought he'd feel again.

Hope.

Then he was falling, the asphalt rushing up at him like a gray wave. But he put his hands out, catching his own fall.

He put his hands out.

Redd tensed as he raised one hand, flexed it, and then repeated the gesture with the other. His limbs obeyed completely, as did his legs as he got back up. He was in complete control again. He was *free*.

Distantly he sensed the squad approaching, but it

was the movement behind Redd that drew his attention. The Parasite Toilet, heavily damaged but still alive, was trying to scrape its way over the pavement with only one good leg left, sparks spitting from its half-ruined body. It stopped when it realized Redd was looking at it, eyes stretching wide with almost comedic fear. Then its mouth turned down in an exaggerated frown, teeth showing, and ...

CRUNCH.

Redd's foot finished the work Zero's weapon had begun, coming down again and again until the parasite was nothing more than an unrecognizable pile of shattered porcelain, metal shards, and bloody sludge.

Only then did Redd turn back to his squad, just in time to see Spike barreling at him. His friend threw his arms around Redd and lifted him up, letting out a long, exuberant screech of guitar chords before releasing him again. The force of Spike's dropping him shuddered through Redd, but it was a welcome sensation. More of his squad surrounded him, slapping his shoulders with excitement as Redd threw out high fives and thumbs-ups left and right.

Then Zero shoved her way through, still brandishing

the new weapon. She didn't bother with pleasantries, not when there was still work to be done.

Redd would have expected nothing less. He pointed frantically behind him, in the general direction the Toilet army had marched from. *There's more infected that way!*

She nodded and raised the gun. *I got it.* Then she stabbed a finger at him and cast an impatient look at the surrounding squad. *Take him!*

No! Redd yanked his arm away as Spike grabbed it, the Speakerman trying to lead him back toward the Alliance lines. He raised his fists. *I still want to fight.*

Zero put up a patient hand. *I know, but . . .*

She didn't get to finish. An explosion suddenly rocked the earth, throwing Redd into the air and then . . .

REDD WOKE UP.

Above him, a metal ceiling floated, blank and indistinct. But also familiar. The Toilets . . . the cell . . .

No! After being so close to freedom, reuniting with his squad, he was back in the Skibidi Toilet base, the parasite still attached. He tried to sit up, but it was stopping him, not allowing him to . . .

"*Redd!*" Guitar chords screeched as Spike's face appeared over him, hands pressing on Redd's shoulders as he fought to get up from the examination table he was lying on.

Spike . . .

Redd relaxed and looked around. He *was* in a base again, but it wasn't the Toilets'. This was familiar territory, a lab filled with Scientists and other Alliance members. And Zero. And the rest of the squad. One by one, they fought their way into his view. The group was a little banged up, to be sure, but it appeared that whatever had happened, Redd had caught the worst of it.

Figures.

Slowly, making sure everything was working okay, he sat up. Around him, everyone in the lab had turned to watch, stopping what they were doing as if he were the most important thing at that moment. He was glad to be back, glad to be alive and to see his squad all in one piece, but . . . Why did they keep looking at him? Then Zero came forward and clapped him on the back, following it with a thumbs-up. But he didn't truly understand the significance of her gestures until Spike pointed at a nearby screen. On it, a video began to play. At first, it was only of a mix of fuzzy, indistinct hallways, but as the recording began to cycle through, Redd recognized what he was seeing: the feeds he'd managed to broadcast while under parasite control. He saw the Skibidi Toilet lab, the parasite releasing the infected Cameraman who then tried to flee . . . One by one, every piece of intel he'd sent out replayed as, around him, the gathered Alliance forces began to clap.

He looked down, embarrassed, but Spike made an encouraging noise and Redd glanced up again. One of the nearby Scientists held the same sort of gun Zero had used on him to detach the parasite. The Scientist pointed to the replays and then to the gun. *Your intel helped us to make it.*

The screen shifted, became unfamiliar. Live broadcasts now, showing battles where the Alliance were closing in on their infected members. One by one, they were getting rescued, their parasites being detached and destroyed. Then the Lead Scientist came forward and showed Redd her tablet. On it was the schematic of the gun. Next to that was another version of it—similar, but much, much larger. Meant to be used *on* something much, much larger.

Redd looked up hopefully.

Yes. The Lead Scientist nodded. *We're going for it.*

THE LAST TIME THE ENTIRETY OF THE BASE HAD gathered in the hangar, they'd witnessed something horrible: the infection of the Titan Speakerman.

This time, the energy was high with anxious anticipation. Spike shuffled nervously beside Redd, hating the wait as much as any of them did. Every Cameraman and Speakerman that could be spared was packed into the space, many standing on the same crates that he and Spike had used the first time to get a better view. They didn't need to resort to climbing anything this time though; they were situated near the very front of the room, waiting as the Alliance leaders on the raised platform before them conferred and communicated with the forces out battling the Toilets. Zero was with the leaders, standing a little off to one side with her arms crossed, as if she was uncomfortable with the elevation in status. Redd didn't envy her; he'd been invited up to the stage as well, but by now, he'd had every member of the base congratulate or thank him at least twice. That was more than enough attention for a while. And besides, he'd spent so much time away from his squad that it was good to be back among them. They seemed to understand this, forming a barrier around him, treating him like he was any normal Cameraman, never mind that the intel he'd managed to broadcast had been instrumental in helping the Scientists develop the Parasite Disabler Gun.

And the new weapon, which—fingers crossed—would see the Titan Speakerman freed soon as well.

A sudden flurry of activity drew everyone's attention to the front of the room, where the large screen burst into life. It was nighttime, the glow from burning fires illuminating the current battle taking place between the Alliance and the Skibidi Toilets. But the fight wasn't the center of attention; the Alliance had been trying for days to lure the Titan Speakerman out into an open area and—finally—it seemed they'd managed to do so. On the feed, the Titan Speakerman appeared, perched at the very tip of a building, firing at the unseen targets below. Despite the Titan's imminent freedom, Redd still felt sick seeing this—he understood better than anyone here what it felt like to be forced to hurt the ones you called friends and allies.

But that revolt shifted to pure hope as the feed turned toward a vehicle screeching its way around a building and onto the battlefield. This is what they had been waiting for: the arrival of the Parasite Disabler Cannon, mounted on the back of the armored vehicle. Throughout the hangar, every Speakerman let loose a wail of excitement and every Cameraman pumped their fists in the air and jumped up and down.

But Redd was barely aware of it. He could only watch the screen as the Cannon charged up its power cells, taking careful aim as it did. Throughout the hangar, the gathered audience held their collective breath.

Then the cannon fired.

Redd's fists clenched in triumph. It was a perfect shot, he could see that immediately, headed directly toward where the Titan Speakerman was situated . . .

Suddenly a Toilet appeared. And no ordinary Toilet. Not even a Giant Toilet.

It was G-Toilet himself, leader of the invaders and the most powerful foe the Alliance had ever encountered. The shot hit him dead center but dissipated immediately without doing any damage. G-Toilet wasn't even *stunned*. Without missing a beat, he turned and fired his laser cannons at the disabler vehicle. It exploded, going from a tool of liberation to twisted, smoking scrap within the space of a heartbeat.

A stunned silence fell over the hangar as, in the feed, the Toilets advanced on the Alliance forces. A moment later, the screen went black.

Redd's fists, tense with excitement only seconds ago, tightened even more with frustrated rage. Around him, the silence broke as Cameramen began stomping their feet in anger and the Speakermen wailed in distress. On the platform, Zero simply hung her head, defeated. They'd been so close. A little longer, that's all they'd needed. If G-Toilet had been even a second slower, the Titan Speakerman would be free now of the evil parasitic Toilet control.

But he wasn't. And until that happened, he was still the enemy.

But it *would* happen. Redd looked up, resolve filling him in a way it hadn't since he'd managed the first broadcast from the Toilet base. He stomped over to the stage and climbed onto it so everyone in the hangar could see him clearly. He held up his hands, waving for attention. Within moments, the room had quieted again. As Redd dropped his arms, he wondered what he was trying to communicate. He wasn't sure, only that he needed to do something to remind everyone here that even though this attempt failed, it wasn't over.

Redd pointed to the screen they'd all been watching, then to the back of his neck where the parasite had been. Then finally to himself.

I'm still here. He tapped his chest to emphasize that point. *There's still a chance as long as the Titan Speakerman is alive.*

He knew what it was like to feel hopeless. To despair. And despite all that, he was standing here today, surrounded by allies, saved because neither he nor his friends were willing to give up. Redd swept his hands in a horizontal cutting gesture, then balled them into fists. *We don't stop. We keep fighting.*

Suddenly Zero was beside him, pumping a fist. Spike joined, nodding his speaker head as his favorite song began to play, loud and encouraging. Below, the onlookers stood a little straighter, some clapping their hands or adding their own gestures of solidarity.

They'd failed this time. But that was today.

None of them were going to stop going. None of them were going to stop fighting.

Not until the Titan Speakerman was free and every single Skibidi Toilet was destroyed.

PART 2:

SCATTERED THREATS

The war rages on. Titan Speakerman remains in thrall to the Skibidi Toilets, much to the frustration of the Alliance. There is a glimmer of hope though. Thanks to the hard work of the Alliance Scientists, utilizing vital intel gathered by a brave Cameraman, the Skibidi parasite threat has been diminished. Efforts to free Titan Speakerman have continued. Intelligence suggests he is being held captive between battles, but the locations remain elusive. Consensus is that more assertive measures to locate and liberate the Titan are needed.

THE HEAT DIDN'T SEEM TO BOTHER THE SKIBIDI Toilets, because no matter how hot the sun got as it roasted the edge of the city, turning the tangle of asphalt highways there into shimmering griddles, the Toilets kept on coming. Plungerman stood at the broken edge of a roadway, fists tight as what little breeze there was rippled through his trench coat. Like cockroaches out of a nest, he thought; an apt comparison, considering how small they appeared from the overpass where he and a contingent of

Alliance members, including his fellow Cameramen, were camped out. A series of explosions sounded in the distance—*pop pop pop*—quick and sharp as bursting balloons, seeming like hardly anything from this vantage point. But given the plumes of smoke that billowed out from between the heavily damaged, nearly skeletal skyscrapers, it was a solid bet that—whichever side had set them off—the munitions had done some damage.

Plunger hoped they were Alliance bombs. Pictured a field of smashed toilets and blank alien eyes and was pleased by it; even wished he had a few grenades in hand right now, to drop down on the unsuspecting Toilets passing by on the streets.

Death from above, you alien scum. They would never see it coming.

But right now he only had his trusty plungers, one of which he held, slapping the handle into his palm over and over with impatience. The weapon was better than an explosive anyway; it was much more satisfying to see the Toilets die up close.

There was another explosion, a lower, louder sound that carried farther than the previous ones. Maybe a missile strike, or a vehicle that had taken its last ride. There was no knowing. Plungerman pulled out a handheld scope from his pocket and scanned the cityscape. More smoke, some fluttering bits of debris, but that was all he could see. No view of the streets, where the worst of the fighting would be happening, or even the particular reason they were out here in the first place, baking beneath the merciless sun.

But as he dropped the scope, he caught a bit of movement. Not within the battered metropolis, but rather at the boundary, where the highways became more open road than city thoroughfare. At first, he expected more Toilets, reinforcements being sent to the front, but the figures were humanoid. Alliance forces, a mixed group of Cameramen and Speakermen. Right away, it was clear they'd taken a beating; several limped along, their clothing singed and torn. A Large Cameraman carried a Speakerwoman over one shoulder, and a Speakerman used a broom as an improvised crutch. They'd definitely seen some real action from the look of them, and unfortunately there was more to come. A handful of Skibidi Toilets appeared, in rapid pursuit.

Plunger's fingers tightened around the handle of his weapon. The Alliance group well outnumbered the Toilets, but given their injuries, it would still be a toss-up. He'd taken a few steps to the edge of the overpass, ready to find a way down to them, to make sure the odds favored the right side, when a hand grabbed his arm.

Plungerman stopped and looked sharply at the Cameraman Scientist beside him, who was shaking his head slowly.

We watch, the gesture said. *We don't interfere right now.*

If it were any other Cameraman making that suggestion, Plunger would have shaken him off, already been halfway to helping the busted-up squad. But 1337 was about as smart as they came among the Alliance Scientists, and he was, for the most part, right about most things.

That didn't mean Plunger had to like it. He disengaged himself, moving so he had a better view of the fleeing Alliance unit, but by the time he got to the edge of the overpass, both they and the Toilets had disappeared from view. So much for that. They were on their own now; he could only hope that their injuries wouldn't keep them from flushing a few more of the Toilet enemy.

Tamping down his frustration, Plunger returned to 1337, who was swiping through Cameraman feeds via the tablet he carried. The two of them might not be part of this fight, but they could observe it. Which was, in fact, the whole point of this assignment.

It wasn't looking good. On the feeds, there were a whole lot of Alliance forces down, their motionless shapes littering battle-scarred streets still teeming with Skibidi Toilets. A pair of Alliance vehicles had been burned to blackened husks; a group of Strider Toilets had cornered a Large Cameraman and were readying to dispatch him. Plungerman's shoulders tightened as a massive shadow suddenly passed over the group, cast by the principal reason that the Alliance was losing this fight.

Titan Speakerman.

The feed they were watching left the doomed Large Cameraman and turned upward, tracking the Titan as it flew across the sky, winding around a skyscraper before landing in the midst of the battle once more. After that, it was basically over. Compared to Titan Speakerman, everything that was left of the Alliance forces was nothing more than a scattering of toys strewn around the behemoth's feet. Despite that, the Cameramen and Speakermen kept fighting, firing their laser guns and flushing any Toilet that got close enough, heedless of the colossal threat they could not hope to overcome.

Because it was all part of the plan.

It was going to be a costly scheme, Plunger noted, as the feed changed again. This time, the angle was much higher up, being broadcast from a building rooftop close to where Titan Speakerman stood as he attacked, his lasers mowing through the figures that should have been his allies. The Titan's back was centered within the frame, specifically his neck, where the parasite that controlled him was still calling the shots despite the best efforts of the Alliance. A red circle blinked in the corner of 1337's tablet; they were recording every moment of this feed, hoping it would offer a fresh clue or unthought-of solution to ending the parasite's control.

Suddenly a gloved hand appeared and snatched the tablet away. 1337 stiffened, but Plungerman wasn't the least bit surprised at who the bold party was. TV Woman now gripped the device, eyeing the screen with the overly casual interest that Plunger had come to associate with the entire TV contingent.

Hey! Plunger jabbed a finger at the pilfered tablet. *We were watching that.*

She ignored him, much to Plunger's annoyance. He'd been skeptical enough when TV Woman deigned to accompany them on this venture, a sentiment that turned to irritation as she lingered at the fringe of the gathering, not seeming to care how many of their allies were falling, barely a klick or two away, in service of their mission. It was only now that she took interest in what was happening. Nearby, 1337's posture was one of uncertainty, a hand held out like he was trying to ask for the tablet back but was too afraid to force the situation. Plunger had no such qualms. He stalked over to her, reaching for the tablet.

But TV Woman lightly stepped out of his reach, pulling the device to her chest as a playful :3 emoticon appeared on her face's TV screen. "*.kool resolc a detnaw tsuJ*"

Plunger held out a hand again, more demanding this time. TV Woman shrugged but relented, passing the tablet back over.

Suddenly one of the Speakerwomen nearby squawked with alarm. Plunger looked up sharply, then followed her line of sight to find a set of spindly legs appearing over the edge of the overpass. Great. A Strider Toilet. At first he thought they'd been discovered, but the Toilet's features went wide with surprise as it pulled itself over the barricade and spotted them. It had just gotten lucky.

Or not.

Plungerman raised his plunger and threw; the weapon landed a direct hit on the Strider Toilet's face, unfortunately not in time to fully stop the cry of warning it emitted, only cut it off. But the force of the blow launched the Strider off the edge of the overpass and sent it plummeting to the street below. By the time Plunger reached the barrier and looked over, the Strider was nothing but a scattering of broken pieces, a lone plunger lying in their midst. Half a dozen grunt Toilets surrounded the remains, staring with puzzled expressions on their warped human faces. Finally one thought to look up. It spotted Plungerman, its features shifting from bewilderment to anger.

1337 appeared at Plungerman's side, tense with concern. But Plunger wasn't bothered, even as the Toilets began racing up the off-ramps toward them. He'd had more than enough of just watching; it was time to have some fun.

He shoved 1337 back, gesturing decisively. *Keep recording the feed and stay out of the way. I'll handle this.*

Still gripping the tablet, 1337 gave him a thumbs-up. *You got it.*

Around them, the rest of the Alliance members readied for the incoming threat, fists raised and weapons in hand.

All except TV Woman. Arms crossed, she stood off to one side, as if annoyed at the inconvenient timing of the attack. As the Toilets appeared from around a bend in the curving asphalt, she waved a hand dismissively. "*.siht eldnah nac uoY*"

A moment later, she was gone, disappearing into a haze of black.

Plungerman's fists tightened. Leave it to a TV to bail when there was actual fighting to do.

Not that he needed her help. He pulled his other plunger from the holder and ran at the closest Skibidi Toilet, slamming the weapon into its face with such force that it spun around bodily, offering him a perfect position to flush it into oblivion. It screeched as it was sucked down into its bowl, the sound muffled by Plungerman's weapon, but no less satisfying for that. He moved on to his next target, kicking at the pale, rubbery visage that snarled at him. His foot landed with an audible crunch, red-flecked teeth scattering across the asphalt. The damaged Toilet lurched back and forth, stunned, as Plungerman kicked again, relishing the feeling of that alien flesh giving way. But this wasn't just about fun. They also needed to make sure this whole group was wiped out. If even one got away and informed its superiors that an odd group of

Alliance members were doing who-knows-what while there was a battle taking place nearby, it would be a problem. Stupid as the Toilets were, that would raise suspicions for sure.

Plungerman flushed the Toilet he was fighting, then finished off another tangling with a nearby Cameraman. He didn't even take the time to return the thumbs-up his thankful comrade flashed him before moving on to the next approaching enemy.

And then, almost as quickly as the scuffle had begun, it was over. The Cameramen did a quick sweep of the area, including scanning the roads below—one retrieved Plungerman's weapon, more than a little excited to do so—then gave the group a thumbs-up. *All clear.*

Back to the matter at hand. Plungerman returned to 1337, who was so engrossed with his tablet that he didn't even seem to notice that they were no longer being attacked. As soon as he was close enough, Plunger saw why.

The Cameraman's feed they were watching had gotten nearer to the infected Titan than ever before—so close to Titan Cameraman's neck that it almost seemed like they'd be able to reach out and touch it. Or attack what was clamped there, folded in on itself but impossible to miss. Something exploded a moment later; the vision wavered and swept down, revealing exactly how the excellent vantage had been achieved. The Cameraman broadcasting it was perched on the narrow ledge of a building, nothing between him and the fall but a few inches of weather-stained stone. But the Cameraman steadied himself, achieving balance once more before his camera moved back to Titan Speakerman, still firing on the troops below.

1337 bounced expectantly, fingers tightening on the device. *Zoom in on the parasite. Zoom in!*

That was clearly the Cameraman's intention, his lens beginning to narrow in. But before he could fully do so, Titan Speakerman spun. His massive visage suddenly filled the screen, menacing energy crackling over the Titan as it took in the unwelcome observer. Either frozen with fear or brave as they came, the Cameraman didn't move as the Titan raised his arm.

A moment later, the screen went black.

1337 grabbed his head with frustration, shaking the tablet as he spun and paced across the roadway.

But Plungerman merely clenched his fists again and turned back toward the city. The sound of explosions had dropped off, less smoke filling the air above where the battle was raging. He knew what that meant.

Minutes later, that suspicion was confirmed. Titan Speakerman suddenly appeared between the buildings and took to the sky, already high above by the time his jetpack carried him over their position and out into the desert to the west.

They'd fulfilled step one of the mission. Or close enough. Now it was time for step two.

Plungerman grabbed 1337 and pulled him to the specially outfitted vehicle waiting nearby. *Time to go.*

This is what they had really been waiting for.

THE PLAN HAD COME TOGETHER A FEW DAYS earlier. For the countless time, Plungerman had watched as G-Toilet, with his grisly humanoid features and glowing eyes, appeared at the very last second, blocking the cannon blast that would have rendered Titan Speakerman's parasite inert and turning the Parasite Disabler Tank into a pile of burning, twisted metal. But no matter how many times he saw the sequence of events play out, the same rage gripped him, along with the frustration that he hadn't been there. It's unlikely he would have made a difference in what happened, but oh, the chance to get up close and personal with G-Toilet, to smash those glaring eyes like overripe melons and wipe that cruel smile off the Skibidi Toilet leader's face . . .

He would have given just about anything to have had that chance.

And it was fantasies like that one that kept him from succumbing to impatient boredom as the Alliance leaders went back and forth, back and forth, debating endlessly what should be done next when it came to the infected Titan Speakerman.

Plunger certainly had his opinions, most of which involved a copious amount of aggressive action and would likely end in equal quantities of blood. But no, Alliance high muckety-mucks were all about caution right now. They'd seen the value of quality intel in the development of the Parasite Disabler Guns and Tank, much of it thanks to a new recruit who'd ended up under Parasite Toilet control. The newbie—Redd, that was his name—was even here now, part of a squad that had cycled into the base recently. Plunger spotted him in the loose crowd that was hanging about as the debate raged, standing with a few members of his crew. Didn't look like much, really. Indistinct from half the Cameramen around him, save for a splash of crimson painted onto his camera's carapace. There was still a green look about him, same as many of the Alliance fighters. They'd seen some action, sure—enough to be smart, to understand how things usually went down—but far from a seasoned veteran. Plunger wondered if Redd would make it long enough to earn that distinction. He hoped so.

But survival rates weren't something worth pondering. Fresh recruit or soldier with a hundred battles under their belt, only one thing mattered: fighting as hard as you could and never backing down in the face of a Skibidi threat.

Growing bored despite his best efforts, Plunger scanned the room again. There were plenty of Scientists around, heads low and tight over their tablets as they traded data back and forth. There were also a few TV Men, the latest addition to the Alliance forces. As usual, they were off to one side, on their own, with an air that this was beneath them. Or at the very least, that they had better things to do. Plunger wouldn't deny the usefulness of their abilities—that light blast of theirs scrambled the Toilets like eggs—but that was only when they bothered to join the fight. Which was not often enough, he would have said, if anyone asked him.

The video playing on a large screen suddenly froze, locked in on an image of Titan Speakerman's parasite. It was a fuzzy view, taken from too far away, so indistinct that it would be hard to pick out the parasite unless you knew what you were looking at.

Which they did, of course.

One of the Head Scientists, a Speakerman, pointed conclusively at the frame. The Alliance members surrounding him nodded in agreement.

Plungerman got it. They could try to rebuild the Parasite Disabler Tank, but the Toilets would be expecting that, keeping an eye out for the weapon. Better to plot a new course of action, find some other way to free Titan Speakerman from Toilet control.

The Head Scientist held up his tablet. More data was needed.

A Cameraman Scientist near Plungerman suddenly threw up a hand, waving enthusiastically as he volunteered for the mission. It was 1337. Plunger wasn't surprised; 1337 was smart, tough, and lucky—a good combination. He'd seen his share of battles and come out of more than the Scientists usually did.

The Head Scientist nodded, accepting 1337 as a volunteer. More hands went up around the room, but Plungerman snapped his fingers assertively, drawing the Head Scientist's attention. Then he pulled out one of his plungers, raising it pointedly. *Gonna need brawn as well as brains on this.*

The Head Scientist seemed to agree and gave him a thumbs-up as well.

Not that it mattered. Accepted or not, Plungerman had no intention of being left behind on this mission.

HE'D LEFT THE PARTICULARS OF THE PLAN TO THE Scientists. What mattered to him was the hunt, and it was on.

In the distance, Titan Speakerman was a speck flying through the air toward some unknown destination, piloted by the foul alien creature attached to him. Plungerman raised a hand to shade his lens. The afternoon sun was beginning to get low, a long shadow sweeping behind their vehicle as they sped off-road across the desert landscape. The heat was still in full force though; it was as if they were driving through a furnace. Besides themselves and their target far ahead, Plungerman hadn't spotted a single living thing since they'd left the city behind hours ago. No, that wasn't entirely true. He'd spotted a trio of vultures at one point, circling something that either wasn't alive, or was getting there.

He pressed the pedal of the vehicle harder, as if it could go any lower than the floor, where it already was. Then he shook his head at 1337, in the passenger seat next to him, the Scientist punching occasional pieces of data into his tablet.

Can't this thing go any faster? Plungerman was reaching the end of his patience. No one said it would be easy tracking Titan Speakerman, but the Scientists had assured him that this bucket of bolts could at least keep up with the Titan's airspeed. Apparently they were wrong.

1337 indicated a Skibidi Toilet on his tablet, then pointed at the shrinking form ahead of them and shrugged. *They may have made modifications we don't know about. Made Titan Speakerman's jetpack faster or more powerful.*

Great. Plungerman considered sparing a couple of minutes to stop and throw out any excess weight in a bid to up their rate of pursuit. They had a stash of weapons, along with a crate of grenades, packed as an overly cautious preparation given that there was no knowing what they would encounter out here. But even as he considered the option, Plunger knew it was already too late. Within minutes, the tiny airborne figure that was Titan Speakerman had disappeared.

But giving up was out of the question. Beside Plungerman, 1337 began tapping rapidly at the tablet, making calculations based on the trajectory Titan Speakerman had been following. A moment later, he reached over, adjusting the steering slightly.

Plungerman tipped his head. *Any idea where we're going to end up?*

1337 shrugged noncommittally and turned the tablet. A map filled its screen, covered in lines that Plunger assumed represented the Scientist's calculations, but there was nothing of note that appeared along those paths, only more and more desert, stretching for what appeared to be days' worth of travel.

So then where the heck was Titan Speakerman headed? Plunger gripped the steering wheel harder and kept the pedal to the floor. For hours, they drove, scanning the horizon for any movement, anything that might indicate the Titan's path. But as dusk began to fall, Plunger finally had to accept the truth.

He slammed on the brakes so abruptly that 1337's tablet nearly flew from his hands. The Scientist fumbled and caught it at the last moment, then twisted toward Plungerman. *What are you doing?*

Plunger waved a dismissive hand ahead of them, where the sun was hanging just over the horizon, washing the desert sand in a vibrant mix of oranges and pinks. *This is pointless. We've lost him.*

1337 pointed at the tablet, more insistently. *If we simply keep following—*

Plunger smacked the steering wheel, cutting the Scientist off. *Titan Speakerman is gone.* He jabbed a finger at the path 1337 had flagged as most likely, tracing it briefly before hooking off to one side. *He could have changed direction at any time, and we'd have no idea.*

1337 didn't have anything to say to that. He turned away slightly, as if acknowledging that Plungerman was right, but not wanting to admit to it.

Plungerman jumped from his seat, exiting the vehicle and kicking up clouds of ocher dirt as he paced away. Not only had they lost Titan Speakerman, but it would also be dark soon. Who knew what they might find in the desert once the sun went down? Or what might find them? Nothing, probably, that was the whole problem, but it was enough to make him glance back the way they'd come and weigh whether it was time to turn around. Maybe 1337 was right, and the Toilets had added some upgrades to Titan Speakerman that made him faster than the Alliance Scientists had anticipated. If so, they could always upgrade the vehicle in turn, wait until Titan Speakerman was spotted at another battle, and begin this whole operation again.

Giving up was the last thing that Plungerman wanted, but the reality was he didn't have any better options on hand.

He was about to return to the vehicle, throw in the proverbial towel, when he spotted a flash in the distance, something glinting in the setting sun. No, not some*thing*—several things, though they were too far away for him to make out. He ran back to the vehicle, ignoring 1337's questioning look as he fished through the gear and brought out the scope he'd used earlier. It took him a moment to find what he'd spotted again, but when he did . . .

Behind him, a horn blared. Plungerman nearly

jumped out of his coat, spinning around to see why in the world 1337 would make a racket when they were trying to . . .

TV Woman was sitting on the edge of the vehicle, hand poised over the horn. Her black teleporation haze was just clearing behind her, revealing 1337 half out of his seat in shock.

:) appeared on TV Woman's screen, and she gave Plunger a little wave. *"?tsol owt uoY"*

Plungerman threw up his hands in exasperation. *Are you crazy?* He pointed toward where he'd been looking, not waiting for her reaction before bringing the scope up again. What he'd seen were Skibidi Toilets, a small company of them. And until a moment ago, they'd been entirely unaware that they were being observed.

That was no longer the case. Through the magnification of the scope, he could see that each and every ugly face had turned in the direction of the horn.

Worse, the Toilets were now headed directly for them.

Plungerman looked back at TV Woman, glaring.

:o appeared on her screen, followed by @_@. *".spoohW"*

He put his hands out questioningly. *You gonna help*

this time? Then he waved dismissively, as she had back in the city. *Forget it. We can "handle" it.*

TV Woman's screen changed to :(. A moment later, her cloud reappeared, whisking her away.

Plunger nearly chucked the scope after her, but it's not like it would change the outcome. Besides, he had a better place to direct his anger—on the Toilets that were closing in fast. He traded the scope for his plungers, then threw 1337 one of the laser rifles. Thankfully 1337 wasn't one of those brainy Scientists who kept to a lab. He could be counted on in a fight.

Unlike some folks.

Plungerman shoved away his frustration with TV Woman and readied to meet the coming threat. Six—no, seven Toilets were headed their way.

No sweat. He'd handled worse.

He raised a plunger only for instinct to throw him backward an instant before the jetpack-modified Toilet that streaked by would have taken his head off. Cackling manically, it ascended back into the air before looping around to try for another pass.

Eight Toilets, then. Plunger glanced back at 1337, who had the laser rifle raised and was already firing at the flyer. With any luck, the Scientist would pick it off—or at least keep it busy—while Plunger dealt with the rest of the incoming enemy. He lobbed his weapon at the first one that approached, but the Toilet was quick; it dodged the strike, then lunged at Plungerman, snapping like a rabid animal. Teeth tugged at the arm of his coat, but he thrust his other plunger downward, shoving the attacking head deep into its bowl before grabbing the flusher. One down, but two more were on top of him before he had a chance to reorient himself. Luck made the first Toilet overshoot as it sprang at him; the second he kicked so hard that it went tumbling across the desert ground and over the edge of a small gully.

Another Toilet lurched toward Plunger, snapping. Suddenly it jerked to one side as a laser blast scored a glancing blow—not enough to take it down, but enough to give Plungerman a chance to pull the flusher. He waved his thanks at 1337, then grabbed the plunger he'd thrown, smashing it onto the head of another Toilet while sweeping his second weapon across the face of the one behind it. The latter was stunned, the former he flushed.

Three, maybe four down. 1337 burst into his line of vision, pulling the flusher of the stunned attacker. But the Jetpack Toilet, who had retreated out of range, descended again with such speed that it knocked 1337 from his feet, the laser rifle flying from the Scientist's grip. The Jetpack Toilet tried to press its advantage and strike at 1337 again, but Plungerman was faster. He dropped his plungers and leapt, colliding with the flyer and wrapping his arms and legs around it. The Toilet tried to blast off again, to put space between it and the fight, but Plunger's added weight kept it from getting more than half a dozen meters off the ground. The rapid-fire punches he threw at its face probably didn't help much either. It lurched to and fro, attempting to throw Plungerman off with increasingly erratic movements. But he held on tight, sneaking in a blow when the opportunity presented itself. The desperate, flailing head finally tried to rear up and twist toward Plunger, a gambit that forced it to stop bucking. Which was exactly what Plungerman needed. He reached for the flusher and pulled.

One moment the Toilet was keeping them aloft, the next, Plunger was plummeting toward the Earth. He hit the desert floor and rolled, coming to a stop on his back not far from the vehicle. Not the hardest landing he'd ever had, but definitely not the softest either.

Suddenly a gruesome smile appeared above him. The attacker's mouth opened, razor-sharp teeth so close that he knew it was useless to try to avoid them, but an instant later the creature exploded, chunks of grisly bits splattering over him. The remains of the Toilet slumped, heavy but very dead. When Plunger finally managed to shove the ghastly mess off, he found 1337 standing nearby, gripping the recovered laser rifle.

Plunger pointed at the splatter covering him. *You couldn't have done that a little earlier?*

1337 shrugged. *Sorry!* Then he offered a helping hand, which Plunger gladly accepted.

On his feet again, Plungerman looked around. A dead Toilet at his feet, what remained of the Jetpack Toilet not far away. Unfortunately its corpse had collided with their vehicle as it fell, leaving a brutal dent in the hood. Not an improvement, cosmetically speaking, but he didn't sweat it. They hadn't outfitted the rover for a tea party.

Finally he turned toward the lone Toilet remaining, which was frozen in place a dozen steps away, looking around frantically, as if it hoped help would appear at the last moment. No, wait—there were two left; the Toilet that Plungerman had kicked into the gully made a sudden reappearance, limping over the edge of the depression. 1337 raised the rifle again, took aim, and fired.

Back down to one.

Plungerman snatched up his dropped weapons and closed in on the sole survivor of the attacking party. This one was *his*. The terrified Toilet backed away and then attempted to flee, but Plunger wasn't about to let that happen. He raised his weapon and brought it back down in one smooth movement, anticipating the sharp collision of rubber and wood against flesh and ceramic, when suddenly a darkness enveloped him. A moment later, he was on the other side of the Toilet, several meters away from where he'd been.

Confused, he spun around. TV Woman stood behind him.

Plunger punched the air angrily. *What do you think you're doing?*

TV Woman held up a placating hand. ".tiaW" Then she moved toward the Toilet, gazing intently at it. Her screen began to glow, accompanied by a low, resonant humming. The light threw a cone of illumination out in front of her, highlighting the enraptured Toilet caught in its path and sending its twisted features into sharp relief. But as the seconds ticked by, the Toilet's face seemed to relax, turned slack and a little dulled. Finally it turned slowly and began to march forward, headed once again into the desert evening.

Plungerman threw up his hands and kicked at the dirt. *You're letting it get away?*

TV Woman turned to him. (¬_¬) appeared. "... *ti wollof ot gniog saw I, oN*"

He tightened with irritation. But she was right—the Toilet was not only on the move, it appeared to have a destination in mind. One that was in the same general direction its group had been headed, and that Titan Speakerman had been flying in.

1337 was quicker; not needing an explanation, he was already back in the front seat of the vehicle, waving frantically at Plunger and TV Woman to get in before the Toilet got too far.

Plungerman obeyed, making sure to ignore the smug sense of satisfaction that surrounded TV Woman as he did.

THE TOILET TRAVELED SLOWLY. CRAWLING BEHIND their unwitting guide at a pace that seemed almost insulting to a vehicle of this caliber, they followed it for hours. Every so often the Toilet would slow, then pause and glance around as if it wasn't sure where it was, or what it was doing. Each time that happened, TV Woman would leap down from where she was perched in the back of the vehicle and bathe the Toilet in a fresh outpouring of her muddling light. Once that was complete, the Toilet would return to its former dazed condition and carry on, leading them deeper into the desert. They ran dark, navigating by the nearly full moon, afraid any headlights would give away their position. Still, Plungerman kept his scope in hand the entire time, scanning the area around them every few minutes to make sure there weren't any more surprises.

During one of these scans, TV Woman rolled her head in an exasperated fashion.

Plunger responded with irritation. *We need to stay alert.*

She swept a hand around at the empty desert. ".selim rof gnihton s'erehT"

Plungerman hooked a thumb toward the Toilet they were following. *That's nothing?*

".laed gib oN .ereht dna ereh stelioT wef A"

As if *she* would know what was a big deal and what wasn't. He jabbed a finger at her and mimed a cloud of smoke. *Right, you just disappear when the trouble starts.*

TV Woman tensed, then grabbed 1337's tablet. The Scientist was driving, the set of his shoulders betraying that he was uncomfortable with the argument and opting to stay out of it. With a few taps, TV Woman called up a projection of the path he and 1337 had originally been following versus their current one. They'd been close with their calculations of Titan Speakerman's trajectory, but wherever this Toilet was going, if they hadn't changed course they would have missed it entirely.

Plungerman shrugged. *We still don't know if this Toilet is headed for the same place as Titan Speakerman was.*

-_- appeared on TV Woman's screen. Then with increasingly frustrated movements, she brought up a recording showing the aftermath of a recent battle. Dozens of dead Toilets were strewn about, but interspersed between them were an unsettling number of Alliance forces as well.

TV Woman indicated the fallen. *".meht ekil pu dne naht suoituac eb ot retteB"*

Plungerman grabbed the tablet away and rewound the footage, showing the fight that had raged before the scene she'd chosen. He pointed at the Alliance forces punching, shooting, and cutting their way through the seemingly endless Toilet ranks. *They fought.* He moved forward again, to scenes of celebration following the battle. *They won.*

TV Woman's screen crackled with static as she waved a dismissive hand.

Plungerman poked 1337 in the shoulder. *Back me up.*

The Scientist glanced back and forth between them before shrugging. He indicated what they were doing, then made the gesture of a gun firing with his fingers. *Careful intel work got us the Parasite Disabler. It's why we are here now, doing this.*

Plungerman swiped through the tablet again until he found a recording of the Cameraman called Redd, who'd managed to get them that intel. *Only because someone was tough enough to fight hard for it.*

TV Woman looked away, as if uninterested. 1337 tipped his head, acknowledging the point, but in a way that gave away that he still had reservations.

It was clear they weren't going to agree. Giving up, Plunger tossed the tablet on the seat beside him, then nodded at their entranced Toilet captive. *Let's just get this done.*

TV Woman made a fuzzy static sound, almost like a laugh, then smacked him playfully on the shoulder. "*.gnola emac I dalg eb dluohs uoY*"

Plungerman crossed his arms and stared out into

the desert, ignoring the jab. Sure, she'd been helpful in hypnotizing the Toilet so it would lead them to its intended destination—and hopefully Titan Speakerman—but she'd still bailed when it came to taking on the group it had been part of. That's what she didn't get; no matter how smart or clever you were, some fights couldn't be avoided. And if they couldn't, it was better to get in there and help make sure *your* side won, instead of keeping a safe distance and simply hoping you came out on top. Yes, the Alliance needed intel—good intel—if they were going to end the war against the Skibidi Toilets. But he wholly doubted that it was the singular element that would win it for them in the end. He flexed his hands, gloves crusted with blood from the last fight. There was no getting around it—sometimes you had to get your hands dirty too.

Suddenly the vehicle lurched, shaking in a strange way for a few seconds before continuing smoothly again. Plungerman glanced at 1337, who shook his head. *Don't know what that was.* It happened again a moment later, the engine sounds going from a low, even rumble to an uneven, screechy rattle. A loud bang, from somewhere within the front of the vehicle, followed. Then it simply . . . stopped. 1337 tapped at its interior controls, twisting the steering wheel and pressing at the pedals, but it was no use. They'd gone dead too.

Plungerman slammed a hand against the side of the vehicle. *Now what?*

1337 jumped from his seat and went around to the front, Plungerman following on his heels while TV Woman dealt with the Toilet, using her enrapturing light to keep it from leaving them behind.

Plungerman tipped his head questioningly at 1337. *What is it?*

He shrugged. *Good question. I have no idea.*

TV Woman came up between them, gesturing pointedly at the dent in the hood, left by the flyer Toilet when it crashed into the vehicle. It had looked like superficial damage at the time, but now . . . 1337 opened the vehicle's front panel, pulling out a small flashlight to inspect the interior. He waved the light back and forth a few times, poked and prodded at the transport's guts, even adjusted some of what lay within. No luck though; the vehicle remained silent and still, a dark lump in the middle of a desert full of dark lumps.

1337 finally turned back, shoulders slumped.

Plungerman waved a hand. *You can't fix it?*

Shaking his head, 1337 reached into the interior and pulled out a part. Plungerman had no idea what it was, but it was clear from the freshly sheared section of metal on one end that it was broken.

Great. That was the last thing they needed. Plungerman suppressed the urge to give the vehicle a good kick, instead stamping out a few meters into the quiet desert. They'd already been moving slowly; having to keep going on foot would reduce their progress even further.

TV Woman came up beside him, a :(on her screen. ".*yrt doog a saw tI*"

Not good enough. Plungerman glanced back at 1337, who was dutifully marking their location on the tablet's map, recording where they had been heading and where their progress had been stalled. He'd clearly given up as well, looking expectantly at TV Woman to teleport them back to Alliance territory.

No. Plungerman slashed a hand through the air. *We aren't done yet.* They still had the Toilet; it could still lead them to where it was headed.

TV Woman rolled her head with exasperation. ".*gniog s'ti raf woh aedi on evah eW*"

That was true. It could be another hundred miles,

or two. Or they could be minutes from reaching their captive's destination. There was still a chance that this mission could bear some fruit, and he wasn't ready to let go of that quite yet. Plungerman pointed to the sky, where the moon hung within the clear field of stars, then at the horizon. *We go until morning.*

1337 looked a little unsure, but agreed. TV Woman was the crux of the matter though. If she decided to disappear on them, he and the Scientist would have a very long, very hot walk back to the city.

But she tipped her head grudgingly as ✔ appeared on her screen.

Soon they were on the move again, trailing the Toilet at a safe distance, just in case its reprogramming faded suddenly. 1337 had the laser rifle slung on one shoulder and Plungerman had his plungers, but they left everything else behind with the dead vehicle in order to travel light, including the crate of grenades, save for a couple that Plunger stuffed in his pockets. The moon slid lower as they walked, with only the sound of their steps crunching over the dry soil to keep them company. Occasionally there was a flash of movement—one of the small lizards that scampered over the rock clusters now that the sun was down, but they were there and gone in an instant. Otherwise, their small strange party was entirely alone.

After a couple more hours, the landscape shifted from flat to a more hilly terrain—not exactly ideal, as it was difficult to see what they were coming up on. But that merely added to the caution Plungerman exercised, once again using the scope to keep watch.

Suddenly he held up a hand. *Stop.*

They'd come to the crest of a hill that sloped down gently to a shallow valley below. What lay there was definitely not the repetitive desert fare they'd seen so far—it was speckled with tiny pinpricks of electric light, which were just enough to trace the dark outlines of several buildings that stood in the valley center. There weren't many, but one was quite large, a huge structure with a curved roof that stood at least four stories high. 1337 pointed, indicating darker stripes of gray crisscrossing the wide-open space in front of it, and Plungerman finally realized what they were seeing: the remains of an old airstrip, neatly hidden by the swell of hills that surrounded it.

While they were taking in the scene, the hypnotized Toilet kept moving, thumping down the hill toward an airfield. Quickly but carefully, Plungerman caught up and flushed it, hoping its movement hadn't been spotted by any of its companions that might be keeping watch. Then he gestured for 1337 and TV Woman to back out of sight. All three ducked behind a nearby outcropping of rock, where Plungerman pulled out the scope again and began surveilling the airfield, signaling to TV Woman to be ready to teleport if there were any signs of impending discovery. It wasn't until a quarter of an hour of nothing had passed before he finally relaxed.

As much as he generally preferred to jump into action, this was a situation that called for caution. Silent, they observed a while longer, taking note of any movement, of which there was little. Sentry Toilets would appear every so often, making their way around the perimeter of the field, but the patrol was perfunctory. It was clear that they didn't expect the Alliance to come this far out and discover their little outpost. At the same time, Plungerman was confused. Why bother with the run-down remains of an old airfield? The walls of the hangar were weather-stained and rusted in spots, the runways too cracked and pitted by the desert heat to be useful for much of anything. Something was up, though, if the Toilets would bother coming this far out themselves. And they needed to find out what.

Plungerman outlined the plan: They would approach together, utilizing a nearby gully to remain out of sight as much as possible. It wasn't great cover, but they'd have to count on the veil of night to cover them, and hope that the patrols they'd seen kept to their schedule. It was also slow going, the little trench filled with gravelly stones and uneven footing. More than once they had to throw themselves to the ground following a loose shower of pebbles, praying that none of the Toilets below had heard the sound. But eventually they made it to the outermost building of the airfield, hardly more than a shack that had seen much better days. Its windows were broken, allowing Plungerman an unimpeded view through the structure all the way to the front of the hangar. One of the patrolling Toilets disappeared around its edge, heading in the opposite direction from them. There were more he couldn't see—and between here and the hangar, the cover was basically nonexistent—but they couldn't wait much longer. Darkness was their friend, but dawn was approaching, and they had an hour or two at best before it would arrive and see them even more exposed than they were now.

Plungerman crept around the edge of the shack, sweeping the area one last time before he waved them forward. They kept low and moved quickly across the pitted asphalt, their shadows sliding alongside them like ghosts. The hangar had two massive bay doors, but Plungerman angled the group toward a smaller portal, what looked like a maintenance entrance just around the corner from the main ingress. As they reached it, Plunger became aware of a faint noise, growing quickly. Definitely one of the patrolling Toilets, the sound coming from the other side of an outbuilding not far from where they stood. They had to get inside, and fast. The gray metal door was right there, but there was one little problem: There was no telling what they'd find on the other side. One Toilet outside, maybe a hundred within. Except the approaching sentry was far enough away that it was unlikely they'd be able to flush it before it raised the alarm. And even if they did manage that unlikely accomplishment, how long before the sentry was missed?

It was a risk either way. 1337 shifted nervously from one foot to the other while TV Woman remained at alert, no doubt preparing to teleport if there was no other choice. Both were waiting for Plunger to make the call.

So he did, reaching for the metal doorknob and

praying that it wasn't locked. But the knob turned smoothly. As the sounds of the approaching Toilet sentry grew louder, Plungerman practically shoved the pair inside, catching the smallest sliver of white appearing around the outbuilding before following and pulling the door shut as quietly as he could.

Had it seen him? For a moment, Plunger remained gripping the doorknob, anticipating a commotion, but there was nothing. Finally he turned to see where they had found themselves.

Luck was on their side for once. Just beyond the door, a high pile of crates was stacked, shielding them from the sight of anyone—or anything—that might be within the main body of the hangar. Using the metal containers for cover, they carefully peeked around into the open space beyond. The sight waiting for them was worse than Plunger could have imagined.

They'd found Titan Speakerman.

But instead of up and moving, the Toilets had him sprawled out on his back on the concrete floor of the hangar, sedated somehow, with a jumble of equipment surrounding him. Countless wires crisscrossed over him, head to toe, feeding into monitors and control consoles. 1337 had been right about the Toilets messing with the Titan; a dozen Researcher variants puttered around the giant, checking readings and babbling among themselves in their grating alien language. A few worked to repair the damage incurred during the latest fight, but for the most part, it was clear that whatever the Toilets were doing, it was for their own benefit. Plungerman felt sick; what they were inflicting on the Alliance's strongest warrior was unconscionable. But also not surprising. It was common knowledge now that the Toilets experimented on their captured rivals, doing who knows what as they pulled them apart into tiny pieces. Still, it was somehow worse to witness it at this scale, with this towering figure, who had been such a beacon of hope within the Alliance.

Yet, as horrifying as the scene was, 1337 kept craning his neck and inching closer to the edge of the crates, trying to get a better view. Plungerman traced where his attention was focused: He was staring at the Titan's head—no, the back of the Titan's neck, which was raised off the floor, shoulders suspended by thick cables. In this position, the Skibidi parasite would certainly be exposed, in a position more vulnerable than it had ever been out on a battlefield.

Which meant that maybe they could free Titan Speakerman here and now.

Plungerman grabbed 1337's arm insistently, turning the Scientist toward him. *Could you do it? Get that creature off him?*

1337 looked at Plungerman, then to Titan Speakerman again, and finally back to Plungerman, tipping his head, unsure. *Maybe.* But then he nodded, a slow confirmation that quickly turned more confident. *Yes, I think so.*

TV Woman's screen brightened briefly. :) appeared.

It was decided, then. They were going to do this. Forget the intel; the only thing they needed to know was that they had a chance to break the Titan away from Toilet control and they were going to take it.

Now all they needed was an opening. That would be easier said than done, given the number of Researcher Toilets crawling around Titan Speakerman's exterior like bugs, but not impossible. What Plungerman didn't see was many soldier Toilets. There were the sentries outside, sure. But other than that, only a handful more of the enemy could be seen, muttering among each other in one corner of the hangar bay.

What they needed was a distraction, something that would draw the Toilets' attention away from Titan Speakerman and, ideally, out of the hangar, giving Plunger and 1337 a chance to get close to the parasite. He touched the outside of his pocket, feeling the hefty object within.

An explosion would do the trick. Plungerman brought out one of the grenades he'd pocketed, handing it over to TV Woman before pointing back outside. Then he indicated the line of piled supply crates that ran along the side of the hangar they were on. She would be the distraction while he and 1337 used the cover to make their way to the other end of the hangar and loop around to Titan Speakerman's neck. They'd have to be fast, but if they got it right, the whole operation could be over in a matter of minutes.

TV Woman accepted the grenade enthusiastically, •~* appearing on her screen.

Plungerman gave her a thumbs-up, followed by two fingers in the shape of a V. *Two minutes. Let's go.*

She nodded, disappearing into her black haze. He and 1337 didn't waste a second. Keeping careful watch at the Toilets' positions, they darted from pile to pile, moving quickly and staying low. It hardly seemed to matter; the Researcher Toilets were engrossed with their work, and the others moved around with an ease that suggested they weren't even considering that their remote outpost had any risk of being infiltrated.

All good news for him and 1337. They reached the final stack of crates, tucked into the corner of the hangar. From here it was a straight shot to Titan Speakerman's head; they could see the profile of the parasite, fully exposed and in a perfect position for 1337 to attempt to disable it. And if that didn't work, well . . . Plungerman pulled one of his plungers from its holster. Physically removing the parasites seemed to work with the smaller ones. He couldn't be positive it would be the same for these larger, more elaborate versions—that a violent removal wouldn't damage the Titan in some way—but he was sure about one thing: It was too dangerous to have Titan Speakerman as their enemy.

No, he was sure of two things. The second was that the Titan would never knowingly help the Toilets, and that he'd rather be reduced to a pile of scrap than be their puppet. Plungerman touched his second grenade through the fabric of his coat. That was a last resort, but if push came to shove . . .

1337 gave him a thumbs-up. *Ready.*

All they needed now was the distraction.

They crouched, ready to spring into action the

moment the explosion occurred. Another minute passed, then two.

Nothing.

Had TV Woman been discovered? Or—Plungerman couldn't help the thought that rose up—had she encountered some obstacle and decided it was a safer bet to retreat?

Suddenly a metallic screech sounded and the hangar doors began to open. That had to be a bad sign. He watched as the ingress grew larger, expecting at every second to see the Toilet sentries herding TV Woman inside, slated to join Titan Speakerman in being experimented on.

If only that were the case. Instead, dozens of Toilets appeared—standard grunts, Striders, a few Jetpack Toilets, and even a larger camo-covered variant—escorting a series of cages on rolling platforms. Those cages were filled with Alliance fighters, Cameramen and Speakermen clinging to the bars or slumped in the corners, nursing injuries.

Plungerman crouched lower, trying to sort out what was happening. Beside him, 1337 jumped suddenly as TV Woman teleported back to where they were positioned, a very worried :(on her screen. She brandished the grenade and Plungerman understood.

She hadn't had a chance to set it off, or hadn't dared to, given the new influx of enemies and the possibility of endangering the captives. But the rest of it didn't make any sense. All of the visible scientific gear seemed both engaged with and specifically tailored to Titan Speakerman. So why would the Toilets bring normal prisoners here? If it was simply for extermination, they could have done that anywhere and not bothered with the cages in the first place.

The answer to this question soon became evident. The newly arrived Toilets steered the cages into an open area of the hangar where markings covered the floor: a large rectangle surrounded by a yellow-and-black chevron border. Plunger hadn't paid much attention to the markings before, figuring they were as much of a relic as the rest of the hangar, but as soon as the cages were within the boundary, surrounded by their Toilets guards, a loud Klaxon sounded. That was followed by the appearance of flashing lights set along the chevron border, as well as a low hum that reached all the way to where Plunger and the others were hidden. Slowly the floor began to sink, the space within that boundary some sort of platform. Light filtered up from wherever it was descending into, along with a few puffs of hydraulic steam. The vibration ceased for a minute, then started up again as the platform ascended back into place, now empty of its passengers.

A hand fell on Plungerman's shoulder—1337's, his attention still fixed on the center of the hangar but his silent message coming through loud and clear.

This changed everything.

They'd thought they'd stumbled upon a simple outpost, a location outfitted with just enough tech to repair and dissect Titan Speakerman, but they'd been wrong. There was clearly something more to see here.

But at the same time, whatever it was, it wasn't their mission. Plungerman gestured toward the prone Titan again. There may be more enemies present now, but they'd disappeared underground. As long as the newly arrived Toilets remained there, it was still possible for them to draw the Researcher ones away, strike quickly and decisively, and . . .

1337 shook his head, then pressed a hand to the concrete floor, urging for the others to do the same. Annoyed, Plungerman indulged the Scientist, feeling nothing at first. But then it was there—a very slight vibration, not unlike the one the platform had given off and barely perceptible through the thick floor, but definitely there. It was the sort of thing you might feel when a lot of electronics, and the power generators needed to run them, were present.

1337 tapped the floor insistently. *The Alliance needs to know what's going on here.*

He wasn't wrong. As much as Plungerman wanted to free Titan Speakerman, if they did that, the Toilets would know this location had been found. By the time the Alliance sent forces to infiltrate, the whole operation could have disappeared, leaving a mysterious—and dangerous—gap in their intel.

TV Woman had similar thoughts. She hooked a thumb behind her, black haze beginning to gather. *".siht troper ot deen eW"*

This time, it was Plungerman who disagreed. *No.* It was the same risk. If they left now, they'd be gambling with whether the Alliance would make it back in time to do anything worthwhile. Not to mention they'd have no idea what they were in for.

TV Woman thumbed behind her again, more urgently.

Plungerman dismissed her with a wave. *Go, if you want. We're staying.*

He put out of his mind that she was their only reliable way out of here if things went sideways. She obviously knew this too, crossing her arms, one hip jutting out with annoyance. But TV Woman remained where she was.

Decision made, what they needed to do now was find a way to reach whatever lay beneath them. The platform was the obvious option, but it was in the middle of the hangar with zero cover. Even with a distraction, it would be nearly impossible to reach it, figure out its controls, and make the descent before they were spotted. And "nearly" was being generous. But if there really was some larger facility hiding below their feet, certainly there was more than one way to access it.

1337 seemed to be having the same thoughts, because suddenly he began pointing at other locations in the floor, at other sets of markings, including a group just beyond the crates where they were hidden. Plungerman kept watch as 1337 leaned out, half exposed as his hand probed what appeared to be some sort of metal handle, painted gray so that it didn't initially stand out from the concrete around it. There were some black marks as well, scratched off to the point of being unintelligible, but when 1337 finally finagled the handle upward, a seam appeared in the floor.

A hatch! But that was all they managed to discern; a Toilet suddenly began turning their way, forcing Plungerman to grab 1337 by the collar and yank him back out of sight an instant before he would have been spotted.

This wouldn't do. A hatch meant some sort of access, but getting all three of them within it would certainly draw more attention than they needed. Teleporting wasn't an option—there was no telling what lay beneath. For all they knew, G-Toilet and a hundred of his minions could be down there. They needed to pause in this effort, take a few minutes and think it through before deciding on how to proceed.

Plungerman turned to TV Woman, to see if she had any ideas.

But TV Woman was gone.

A moment later, a loud crash rang out. Across the hangar, near the opposite wall, a dusty old shelving unit full of boxes and jars was now lying face down on the floor. The glass jars that had lined its shelves were shattered, sending the screws and washers and other metal bits rolling away like dropped marbles.

TV Woman reappeared, stepping out of her cloud with a great big :) filling her screen. "*!gniog teg s'tel ,lleW*"

Reckless, stupid, and done without warning them.

Plungerman would have given her a piece of his mind if they'd had the time. But they didn't. The crash and subsequent mess had drawn the attention of all the Skibidi Toilets in the hangar, but it was a window of opportunity that was going to close quickly. 1337 went for the hatch, pulling it open to reveal some sort of maintenance tunnel below, thankfully large enough for them to climb into, though it would be a tight fit. The Scientist went first. Plungerman gestured for TV Woman to follow, then climbed in immediately after her, bringing the hatch back down. As it locked back into place, darkness descended, broken only by the occasional blink of tiny lights.

1337 clicked his flashlight on. The ceiling within the hatch space was low enough that they needed to crouch, and even then, their heads skimmed the ceiling. Pipes and bundles of wires, along with a number of circuit panels, surrounded them. The blinking they'd seen was from status lights on those panels, but another faint glow was now visible at the other end of a narrow tunnel that led off from the little space. Given it was the only option, they took it. 1337 had the means of illuminating their path, so he went first, followed by TV Woman and Plungerman, bringing up the rear. The passage was small enough that they were forced to crawl on their hands and knees, and it was slow, less-than-comfortable going.

Luckily the tunnel didn't go far. They reached a vent at the other end of it, a metal panel with horizontal slits in it. With the others in front of him, Plungerman couldn't see what lay beyond this, but after a few minutes, he heard the faint metal twang of the covering being removed. Apparently 1337 had judged the situation safe enough to proceed. Soon they were upright again, in what appeared to be some sort of storage closet. There were more crates here, smaller ones than in the hangar but clearly marked with the strange Skibidi language. Curious, 1337 opened one to investigate, but there was nothing of real interest, mostly common-looking spare parts.

But spare parts for what?

A door led from the room. Cautiously Plungerman opened it a crack. A hallway lay beyond, lit with cold fluorescent lights but otherwise empty. He waited, listening intently for any evidence that there were Toilets nearby, but there was nothing. He waved the others forward, slipping silently into the hall. There was no knowing which way to go, so he chose left, inching down the hallway toward a juncture, where it split again. Here they found a helpful map etched into one wall—simplistic, but it was enough to help them orient themselves. What remained unclear was what kind of base this was. Or if it was a base at all. There were multiple levels, as well as a number of branching hallways that certainly covered a larger footprint below the surface than the hangar did above, but the spot that drew their collective attention was what appeared to be a large chamber, easily ten times bigger than anything else they could see, only a few turns ahead of them. Choosing the hall that would lead there, they kept going—slowly, meter by meter, anticipating that a Skibidi Toilet would appear at any moment and discover them. But despite the size of the facility, it didn't seem heavily infested; they encountered nothing, and heard no sounds beyond the occasional doors they passed.

Finally they came to a long corridor that opened up into a brightly lit space on the other end. Plungerman stopped them before they reached the end of it, slinking along the last stretch of wall and peeking his head out to see what lay beyond.

Their suspicion that this was more than a simple outpost was an understatement. A massive room opened up before him, twice as large as the hangar above. They were near the top of it, the opening they'd reached leading out onto a balcony looking down on a wide-open floor far below. There was a stairway to one side of the balcony, which led down to another below, then crisscrossed over the wall down to a half-level that ran around three edges of the space. It was a strange setup; the balconies seemed to have no other purpose than to serve as vantage points for whatever the space was used for. But whatever that was, Plunger wasn't sure. Its size suggested it might have something to do with the Titan above, but at the same time, that didn't quite feel right.

He waved the others forward, all managing an adequate view without exposing themselves. Though the balconies were empty, the floor below certainly wasn't. The cages full of captured Alliance fighters had been brought here, lined up in a row at the far end of the space. A few of the Toilets who had delivered them still lingered around, acting as guards. Completely opposite, across a stretch that was easily the size of a football field, was a set of arched doorways, all closed. The partial level was also populated, home to long lines of control consoles with screens mounted in the walls above them. There were also more Researcher Toilets here, moving to and fro as they did . . . well, whatever it was they were doing. Compared to their counterparts above, they gave off a more frantic energy, but also more decisive, as if they were preparing for something specific.

Plungerman turned to 1337 and tapped his finger against his camera head. *Start broadcasting. Record it all.*

1337 nodded, fixing his lens on the space below. Then his lens dropped as he thumped the heel of his hand against his head. When he looked back up, he focused on the goings-on again, then shook his head. *No go.* He gestured around them, at the metal walls and whatever secrets might lie within them. *There must be something preventing broadcasts.*

Which meant that the Toilets were being more careful than usual. Maybe they'd learned from the experience with the Alliance's development of the Parasite Disabler Gun. But what, then, exactly, was going on in this facility?

Suddenly a siren went off, one short burst of sound that cut off as quickly as it started. The Toilets guarding the Alliance captives jumped to attention, then clustered around one of the cages. Opening it, they pulled out the closest Cameraman, herding him like an animal to the center of the room. Every time the Cameraman tried to fight back, or to run, one of the Toilets would be there, snapping or prodding as its companions laughed. The worst came when they'd gotten the Cameraman where they wanted him; suddenly one of the Toilets—the Camo Toilet they'd seen earlier, and the only one with mounted weapons—fired two quick shots, each targeted at the Cameraman's knees. In an instant, he was down, writhing in pain as the Toilets retreated to where the cages were. As soon as that happened, a wall of some clear material, tinted slightly blue, rose out of the floor, partitioning their section of the chamber off from the rest.

The Cameraman they'd hobbled wasn't deterred by his injuries though. Plungerman pumped a fist at his side as the Cameraman began dragging himself toward the doors, the only other visible exits on that bottom level. Once again, the Toilets laughed, but despite the pathetic sight, Plungerman quietly applauded the Cameraman's unwillingness to give up.

Then a light over one of the doors turned red. It slid open, revealing a dark chamber beyond. The Cameraman stopped crawling. A moment later, Plungerman saw why: The outline of a Toilet appeared in the door. It exited slowly, almost tentatively, stopping a few paces into the room, still a fair distance from the Cameraman. Meanwhile, all of the Researcher

Toilets had stopped what they were doing and were lined up along the rail of the balcony level.

Plungerman tightened, an apprehensive feeling rising. What was this? Some sort of training for new Toilet fighters? It was hard to get a good read on what was happening; the Alliance did something similar with their captured enemies, but how this was set up sat wrong with Plunger; he just couldn't put his finger on why. It didn't make sense to hobble the Cameraman unless his opponent was particularly weak or untrained, which . . . maybe it was. It certainly appeared like a normal grunt, nothing distinctive about its size or how it was outfitted, except . . .

No, there *was* something different about this Toilet. Plunger hadn't seen it at first, thanks to the high angle they were looking down from, but the eyes of this Toilet were different. They were circled in what appeared to be metal and circuitry instead of normal skin. Plunger glanced at 1337 and TV Woman; they'd noticed the alteration as well. So had the Cameraman below as the strange Toilet began slowly approaching again. Plunger took out his scope and focused in on the creature's eyes; they had some sort of metallic telescoping covering where the eyeballs should have been, through which a tiny bead of red light was visible. It gave the creature an especially sinister look but didn't offer any clues about what the alteration meant. Only when it got close enough to the Cameraman did the eye portals suddenly twist open, the light bursting from them so bright at first that Plunger had to drop the scope. By the time his vision cleared, the injured Cameraman was fully bathed in the crimson light of the Toilet's strange orbs, seemingly fixated in place and entranced in a similar way their Toilet guide had been by TV Woman. Then as the whole of the room looked on—Researcher Toilets, Toilet guards, and captives alike—the Cameraman began to convulse violently, flopping around on his broken body like a fish pulled from water.

It was so appalling that Plungerman didn't even realize he'd take a step forward until 1337 stopped him.

The Scientist shook his head warily. *No heroics.*

Plungerman didn't like it, but 1337 was right. There was nothing they could do now except see how this played out. On the other side of him, TV Woman hadn't even seemed to notice his movement. She was frozen in place, her screen dimmed so that the appalled D: that had appeared on it was barely visible.

Meanwhile, the Cameraman continued to convulse

as the Toilet focused its sickly light on him, the beams from its eyes widening in scope, though its victim's violent motions began to slow. This was bad, Plunger thought. They'd encountered a lot of variations of the Toilets so far, with a wide range of different abilities, but they'd adapted, improving their own weapons and attacks in turn. This modification though—coupled with the fact that it seemed to be applicable even to the most common, weakest Toilets—was unsettlingly disturbing. And far too effective.

Maybe they should have been anticipating something like this. The Toilets were constantly trying as hard to emulate or top the Alliance arsenal as the Alliance was always trying to get one step ahead of them. When the Speakermen joined the war, the Toilets had turned to headphones and other ear coverings to survive their sonic attacks. When the TV Men appeared, they adopted glasses that would render light attacks inert. This was simply the next step—for the Toilets to turn their own versions of these abilities back on the Alliance. And from what Plungerman could see, the Toilet's mesmerizing light covered a far broader area than a TV Person's. With this technology, a single Toilet would be able to render a dozen or more Alliance fighters entirely ineffectual while its companions picked them off. Or worse, scramble them into doing something without knowing it, as TV Woman had done with the Toilet in the desert. And if there were many Toilets with this new modification . . . Plunger shied away from imagining the massacres that would ensue.

Abruptly the modified Toilet's blistering stare began to flicker. The creature's neck stiffened, the head rising above its bowl before beginning to twitch. The vicious light blinked in and out as well, the eye portals opening and closing out of sync. Strangely though, this didn't seem to bother the Researcher Toilets, who simply leaned over the railing as they observed with intensified interest.

Suddenly the modified Toilet's eyes exploded, metal and glass shards twinkling in the air as they rained down on the now still Cameraman. Smoke poured from the Toilet's eyes as its head wavered and then slumped forward over its bowl. When it didn't move again, it became clear that it was dead.

The Cameraman, on the other hand . . .

No longer assaulted by the fierce, incapacitating glow, the crumpled figure began to stir, raising his head and shaking it, as if in a daze. He spotted the dead Toilet, then turned toward the other captives and gave a thumbs-up. They cheered supportively. Plunger couldn't quite share their sentiment. Not when he expected what was about to happen next. The glass wall that had protected the Toilet guards went down and they approached the Cameraman, as if to retrieve him. But their test subject had run out of his usefulness; a moment later, the augmented Toilet wasn't the only body lying in a heap on the floor.

1337 hung his head. Plungerman felt the same. To be forced to watch something like that, unable to do anything . . . but this wasn't over yet. A contingent of the Researcher Toilets had made their way down to the floor and were now inspecting the remains of the augmented Toilet as they babbled among themselves. Following a few minutes of this, one turned and called something up to a Toilet still waiting on the level above. It nodded decisively and went over to one of the consoles, then adjusted the controls there. Finally the Toilet hit a button. A wall beside it slid open, revealing a smaller, hidden room. Within that alcove was a device unlike anything Plungerman had ever seen before. 1337 apparently hadn't either, given how the Scientist moved closer and pawed at Plunger to hand over his scope. The device was about the height of a Large Cameraman and consisted of a round metal platform bolted to the floor, upon which a series of glass lenses were embedded. Spindly appendages reached down from a panel above, with what appeared to be lasers mounted at each of their ends. Finally, standing between these setups stood a glass cylinder filled with a crystal-clear fluid, within which floated dozens of milky glass orbs.

The Researcher Toilet that had opened the wall went over to the strange machine and made a few adjustments, then flipped a series of switches. The appendages suddenly came alive, moving into a ready position. Once they'd locked in, their lasers flared to life and fired into the liquid, specifically focusing on one of the floating orbs. That sphere began to glow, turned slowly from translucent white to a bloody red, at which point the lasers moved on to a second orb. Finally the altered spheres were sucked into the bottom of the cylinder, reappearing a moment later in a metal slot just outside it. The Researcher Toilet collected the orbs, then called down to the others on the floor, who proceeded to gather up the remains of the dead Toilet and drag it back through the door it had originally entered through. As the Toilet with the new set of orbs disappeared through a different door, Plunger could guess what it was on its way to do: install them in the next Toilet test subject.

After all, there were several more cages full of Alliance prisoners to get through.

1337 dropped the scope, his movements agitated.

TV Woman, who'd remained calm and silent so far, let out a faint crackle of static that sounded disgusted, then pointed upward. "*.siht no troper og ot deen eW*"

Plungerman nodded. *We will.* But he remained where he was, staring down at the dead Cameraman, who the Toilets hadn't even bothered to clear away. They'd just left him lying there, like a piece of discarded trash.

"*!woN*" said TV Woman, more insistently.

Plungerman spun at her, jabbing a finger toward the caged Alliance fighters. Thanks to the experiment that had played out before them, every single one now knew what their fate was . . . unless Plungerman and the others did something. They might not have been able to save the Toilets' first lab rat, but he wasn't about to leave the rest behind to die. *We have to help them.*

>:(appeared on TV Woman's screen. "*.tnatropmi erom si noitamrofni ehT*"

They are important too.

".wonk ot sdeen ecnaillA ehT"

Plungerman clenched his fists, ready to argue further, but 1337 slipped between them, hands held up and calling for peace. Then he looked pointedly back at the strange device. *That machine needs to be destroyed.* He pointed at his lens, then sliced one hand through the air. *Before they can perfect the process.*

Three goals, Plunger mulled. All important in their own way, with their own price that the Alliance would pay if they failed to accomplish them.

It was frustrating to admit, but 1337 was right. Destroying the machine was the priority. Doing that was their best chance to delay, or even permanently destroy, this new Skibidi technology development. And the opportunity to do that was *right now*, while most of the Researcher Toilets were no longer in close proximity.

Plungerman reached into his pocket and pulled out the grenade stashed there. TV Woman mirrored that action, handing 1337 the explosive she hadn't gotten a chance to use earlier.

Two grenades. It would have to be enough.

And they'd have to be quick. Down on the scientific level, Plungerman counted the Toilets that still remained. He held up three fingers—one for each of them. 1337 and TV Woman nodded, ready. Moving as quickly and quietly as they could, the trio began descending the stairs, pausing at each balcony to check and make sure no Toilets were in the corridors that ran off of them. 1337 clutched one grenade, Plungerman had the other. He also pulled one of his plungers from its holster, fingers tight around its handle.

They managed to make it all the way down to the balcony just above the scientific level when one of the Toilets there turned suddenly, looking their way. It spotted them, features widening with surprise. Plungerman lifted the plunger and lobbed it like a spear, but it was too late. The Toilet's squawk was cut off by the weapon's direct hit, but its two companions, along with the guards on the floor below, jumped to attention at the sound.

Plungerman slapped 1337 on the shoulder. *GO!* Then he leapt off the edge of the balcony, landing so hard on the floor below that his knees nearly gave out. No time for that; he righted himself at the last moment and took off running, heading directly for the orb-making machine. One of the Researcher Toilets appeared in front of him, attempting to cut

Plungerman off, attacking with a ferocity unexpected for a creature that probably spent most of its time in a lab. Plunger barely managed to dodge in time. But the Toilet had made a mistake in getting so close. Two steps forward and its flusher was within grabbing distance.

That was one Toilet down.

Plungerman held the grenade tighter and began running again. The orb machine was directly across the chamber from where he stood, but it was too far for an accurate throw, forcing him to follow the horseshoe shape of the level they were on and try to get closer. The stairs came out ahead of him; 1337 and TV Woman had already reached the bottom. 1337 was tangling with one of the remaining Researcher Toilets while TV Woman was on her way toward the Toilet with a plunger still stuck on its face. She grabbed the weapon's handle, using it to aggressively shove the flailing head into the depths of its bowl before yanking its flusher. Plungerman glanced behind in time to see 1337 flush his Toilet as well and run to join them.

That left the way to the machine clear.

Plunger signaled them both. *Let's go! Faster!*

Surprise was no longer on their side. The Toilet guards below would be here any moment, along with who knew how many reinforcements from the rest of the base. 1337 ran toward the consoles—they needed to destroy as much of the experiment's data as possible too—pulling the pin on his grenade and rolling it like a bowling ball. The explosive slipped neatly beneath the block of control panels; a few seconds later, they exploded, sending fragments of circuitry flying and leaving nothing left of the computers but a smoking metal shell.

One target down . . .

Plungerman ran for the orb machine, pulling the pin on his grenade and tossing it into the alcove.

The moment it left his fingers he saw what he couldn't have seen from their vantage point above: an additional set of controls, set off to one side of the orb machine and operated by another Researcher Toilet. It lunged as Plungerman threw, catching the grenade in its mouth and bolting, making it to the rail and throwing itself over before any of them had a chance to stop it. The Toilet exploded in midair. The shock wave of the detonation sent them all flying; Plunger collided with a wall so hard that for some indeterminate measure of time, everything went fuzzy. He was on the floor, he realized, as the world sharpened up again, with 1337 and TV Woman lying nearby. They appeared shaken, but unharmed, as far as he could tell.

But confirming that would have to wait. He'd screwed up. The orb machine was still intact and the opportunity to destroy it was rapidly disappearing. He pulled his second plunger, ready to smash the thing into pieces if that was the only option, but the instant he turned toward the alcove, he found a Strider Toilet blocking his way. No, more than one—they were pouring out of the balcony a level above, skittering their way down the wall.

Behind him, 1337 and TV Woman were back on their feet, but more Toilets had appeared beyond them. The guards from below had finally made their way up to the scientific level, effectively trapping the trio.

Plungerman moved closer to the others and gripped his plunger tighter, ready to fight, but TV Woman shook her head.

"*.yzarc er'uoY*" she said. "*.og ot tog ev'eW .dluoc ew tahw did eW*"

Plunger pointed his weapon at the orb machine. *Not while that thing is still functioning.*

TV Woman went tight with frustration, but before she could say anything else, a Strider Toilet dropped down from above, landing between her and where 1337 and Plungerman stood. It grinned gruesomely, white teeth flashing as TV Woman took a nervous step back, stopping when she realized the Toilet guards were closing in from behind.

Plungerman raised his weapon. *Fight!*

Instead, the black haze appeared. A moment later, TV Woman was gone.

Coward! Plungerman swung the plunger with frustrated anger, hitting the Strider so hard that it smashed into the wall, stunning it. But the other Toilets were only steps away and approaching fast. There was no choice now: If he and 1337 wanted to walk away from this alive, they would have to fight their way out. The Scientist readied himself, but with a hesitance in his movements that hinted at the understanding that they were vastly outnumbered; even Plungerman had to admit that.

Unless . . .

He grabbed the Scientist's arm and pulled him to the rail. The cages containing the Alliance captives still lay below, now unguarded. 1337 caught on, though with reluctant acceptance—he understood what Plungerman wanted to do, and that it wasn't going to feel so good. But when Plunger stepped onto the rail and jumped,

1337 didn't hesitate to follow. They plummeted, the floor rushing up far too fast. Plunger tried to stay loose, letting himself roll as his feet hit, but the landing was still hard. Rattled, he lay still for a moment, then forced himself to get up. Thankfully everything was still working. 1337 hadn't fared quite as well. He was up again too, but limping, unable to put his full weight on one knee. Still, he moved determinedly toward the nearest cage. Plungerman caught up, grabbing his arm and throwing it around his shoulder, helping the Scientist close the last of the distance. The enclosure had a complicated-looking digital lock, but 1337, genius that he was, made short work of it and the door snapped open, freeing the Cameramen and Speakermen within.

And just in time. The Toilets had caught up and were approaching from the other side of the testing chamber in full force. Plungerman hoisted his weapon as some of the captives formed a protective circle around 1337, watching the line of enemy draw closer and closer. But 1337 worked fast. Once the remaining Alliance members were freed, their chances for survival—while still far from what anyone might call good—had improved significantly. All they needed to do was make their way up and out of the facility;

if they could reach the desert, they could scatter, disappear into the hills. They might not all elude the Toilets in the end, but some would.

1337 reappeared at Plungerman's side, bracing himself on his good leg. Plunger felt a twinge of anger, followed by sadness. The Scientist, for all he'd done, probably wouldn't be among those that managed to make it back to the city, not on that leg. If TV Woman were still here, she could have teleported 1337 to safety, but . . .

But she wasn't, and it wouldn't do any good to dwell on that now. At least her cowardice meant someone would inform the Alliance what they'd seen here. He'd definitely be giving her a piece of his mind the next time he saw her though . . . if there was a next time.

Plungerman raised his weapon, signaling to the others to get ready. A moment later, the first wave of Toilets hit. As they did, the Speakermen let out a deep, thumping war cry that echoed off the walls, reverberating in a way that seemed to infuse Plungerman with new strength. A Strider came at him; he landed a punch that crushed its bulbous nose, then smashed it over the head with his plunger. Blood sprayed. As the Strider went limp, Plungerman yanked on its flusher, but no sooner had he done that than a second Toilet attacked, and a third, both normal grunts but dangerous enough in a melee like this. One lurched at Plungerman, sending him stumbling into a Speakerwoman whose sonic attack was interrupted as she dropped to her knees. Plunger pulled her back up an instant before a Toilet landed where she'd fallen; unfazed, the Speakerwoman punched the attacker and flushed it. Plungerman's assailants took another shot at him; he shoved the handle of his plunger into the mouth of one while kicking at the other. A vicious smile turned to a frown as teeth shattered from the blow, then disappeared as the head was sucked into its bowl, thanks to a flush assist from a freed Cameraman.

But that still left the other attacker. Plungerman wrestled with the Toilet, whose jaw had clamped down on his weapon like an iron vise. There was no pulling the weapon free, nor striking a blow with it. So he improvised; he released the plunger and jabbed a thumb into each of the Toilet's eyes. It screamed and dropped the weapon as blood and other fluids burst from its sockets, but its suffering was cut short—though maybe not as short as it could have been—when Plungerman yanked its flusher.

Retrieving his weapon from where it fell, Plunger paused for a moment to take in the battle raging around him. What he saw wasn't good. They were fighting—and well—but it was simply a matter of numbers. Several of the freed Alliance fighters were already down, and though there were twice as many Toilet dead, they simply had more to spare. 1337, thankfully, was still standing, but barely holding his own against the Camo Toilet. It fired its laser at the Scientist. 1337 managed to dodge quickly enough that the shot only skimmed his shoulder, but his knee went out as he did. Now on the floor, with the Camo Toilet looming above him, the Scientist looked up—not at his foe, but rather at Plungerman, who was already running for where his friend was, knowing he'd be too late.

Suddenly there was a massive explosion in the center of the oncoming Toilet horde. Smoke filled the air as metal and viscera rained down throughout the testing room. Injured Toilets cried out and the attackers paused their advance, looking frantically around to see what had happened. Plungerman couldn't help but do the same.

Above, leaning on the rail as if she were watching something as innocuous as a sporting event, was TV

Woman. She gave him a little wave, then pulled another grenade from the case behind her—the case Plunger had last seen on the back of the busted vehicle—and tossed it into the Toilet's midst. Plungerman crouched and covered his head as it went off, then was back up again in a shot. Devastation filled the testing space, but almost entirely on the Toilet side now. A few still continued to attack the captives, but most of the enemy had turned to retreat.

No, not to retreat. They were headed for TV Woman.

Which she'd clearly anticipated. As they closed in, she pulled pins from two grenades and tossed them into the alcove with the orb machine. The Toilets screeched with anger and desperation, but there was nothing they could do now. The grenades exploded, a bright crimson light briefly emanating from the space before going dark. More smoke and debris followed; an orb plunked down a couple meters from Plungerman, then rolled his way. He stopped it with one foot, then brought his heel down on it, feeling it crunch satisfactorily. By the time he looked back up at the rail, TV Woman was gone, but she reappeared beside him an instant later, dragging the crate of explosives.

:P was on her screen. *".tey toN .uoy denodnaba I thguoht uoy, wwwA"*

Plungerman ignored this, gesturing at the alcove above. *It's destroyed?*

".seceip noillim a otnI"

It was the confirmation he needed. Plungerman hefted his weapon as 1337 came limping over, now suspended between two helpful Speakermen. *Let's get out of here.*

Thumbs-up all around.

Plungerman shoved as many grenades into his trench coat pockets as would fit—indicating for the others to do the same—then led the charge, cutting through the center of the carnage toward the only exit the Toilets didn't seem to be paying attention to: the doors at the opposite end of the testing chamber, where the altered Toilet had come through. The Camo Toilet that had shot 1337 lunged as they passed it; Plungerman kicked it away before grabbing its mounted laser and snapping it off. The Toilet screeched, a sound quickly cut off by TV Woman pulling its flusher. That was the worst of the remaining resistance; a few more dead Toilets later and they'd reached the doors. Here the control panel gave 1337 a little more trouble, but they kept the Toilets back, giving the Scientist time to work. Finally a door slid open. Once the Alliance forces were all inside, Plungerman smashed the control panel, sending sparks flying. The door swooshed closed again; he barely managed to dive through it before it locked into place.

The sudden silence was strange. No doubt they still had plenty of fighting to go before they managed to get out of the facility, but for the moment, there was a lull. The Skibidi threat was cut off behind them; they could afford a moment to regather themselves. It took a moment for Plungerman's vision to adjust to the low lighting of the new chamber they found themselves in. It was bigger than he'd expected—nothing compared to what they'd just left but large enough that the low red illumination from a single light in the ceiling didn't reach its edges. He counted a couple dozen Cameramen and Speakermen left, all gathered together as they did a quick inspection of injuries. Fortunately there wasn't anything too bad. 1337's busted knee was still the worst among them, but his new Speakermen assistants kept him upright and ready to move.

With that done, it was time to decide what to do next. It had been a gamble shutting themselves into this unknown chamber, but fortunately there was another door at the other end. Plungerman started toward it.

"*Hee.*"

He froze. The sound had come from the right, out of the depths of the darkness.

"*Hee hee.*" It came again, a cross between what might have been words and a laugh.

A shadowy figure appeared.

They all went on guard, Plungerman ready to turn the Toilet's face into pulp at the hint of any red, but as the lone enemy moved into the dim light, it became clear that the Toilet had entirely normal eyes, with none of the modifications they'd seen earlier.

Plunger relaxed, holding a hand up to the others to stay put as he approached the Toilet. It must be pre-upgrade, maybe even the intended recipient of the freshly made orbs. Well, that wasn't going to happen now. Can't upgrade a flushed . . .

Suddenly the Toilet opened its mouth, revealing metal mesh within, with a single red orb set in the center.

"*EEEEEEEEEEEEEEEEEE!*"

An instant before the onslaught hit him, Plungerman realized what he'd seen: a speaker. Its sound hit like a physical blow, sending him stumbling backward as he threw his hands up to his head, trying to dampen the assault. But that did nothing. He'd felt the power of the Speakermen's sonic attacks before, but this was deeper somehow, more forceful, with a clawed vibration that seemed to shred him from the inside. It was agony. And not only for him—the others were writhing on the floor, rendered utterly helpless by the incessant, unrelenting noise. Some tried to crawl away, but there was nowhere to go; the noise bounced off the walls, filling every corner and crack of the room. His perception wavering, Plungerman saw TV Woman's black cloud appear again, but it was patchy, incomplete. Then it dissipated, TV Woman's screen fritzing back and forth between frenzied static and >o<.

Plungerman had to do something. He'd dropped his plunger somewhere, but his vision kept cutting in and out, making it impossible to find it. He focused on the Toilet instead, on taking a step toward it, then another, and another. Each one brought more pain, more of the thought-scrambling cacophony, until he couldn't even remember what his intention had been. There was only the thunderous, all-encompassing din and a triumphant face—open-mouthed, limned in red . . .

He punched. The blow was wild, desperate, but it connected, hitting one of the Toilet's eyes so hard that it bruised almost immediately. The sound cut off briefly and Plunger tried to gather himself, to finish off the job, but before he could, the Toilet grimaced angrily and let loose once more. The next thing he knew, he was on his knees, barely cognizant of where he was . . . who he was . . . There was nothing but the sound, growing louder and louder and . . .

Suddenly it turned muted. Shaking his head to clear it, Plungerman looked up. 1337 lay nearby, wielding the plunger that Plungerman had dropped. He'd shoved it over the Toilet's mouth, dampening the sound while attempting to use the handle and his one good leg to pull himself off the floor. Straining, 1337 reached for the flusher. But the plunger was already beginning to fail, fissures appearing on its bulb, cracks through which the sound began to leak out. Then, in the space of a heartbeat, it shattered. Plungerman braced himself, but no fresh sonic assault followed.

1337 had managed to pull the flusher. Within the

Toilet's mouth, the red orb had gone dark. Then its head began to spin, faster and faster until it was sucked down into its bowl.

For a moment, all Plungerman could do was stare. 1337 couldn't even do that; he collapsed onto his back, chest heaving from the effort, but Plunger guessed he had the same thoughts running through his head. How many of these altered, upgraded versions did the Skibidi Toilets have? And how close were they to perfecting them? The TV-esque glow had been bad enough, but if the sonic attack had been enough to disrupt TV Woman's teleportation . . . if they were able to push the assaults even further . . .

The Alliance needed to know about all of this. And Plungerman needed to make sure this threat was stopped, here and now. He pushed himself back to his feet and signaled the others. They needed to get out of here as fast as they could. He went to the door, half expecting it to be locked, but it opened easily into a deserted corridor. Good. The remaining Speakermen and Cameramen waited for him to wave them forward, with TV Woman and 1337 bringing up the rear. 1337 was even worse off than before, the occasional spark bursting off of his camera head, his entire body still trembling. He must have taken some sort of internal damage from the sonic Toilet, but exactly how bad it was remained to be seen.

Plungerman stopped them a few steps into the corridor.

He gestured at the Scientist, then TV Woman, and finally pointed up. *Get him outside where it's safer.*

TV Woman shook her head, a little burst of static on her screen. *".em deen uoY"*

Plungerman nodded emphatically at 1337. *He needs you more.*

And they needed to make sure someone was alive to tell the Alliance what they'd seen, with as much detail as possible. He wasn't going to say that TV Woman had been right to try to get them to flee earlier and leave the captives behind, because she wasn't. But what they'd learned since then was crucial additional intel that they couldn't risk dying with them.

He held out a hand, tapping one of his bulging pockets. *Hand over the explosives you have and go.*

TV Woman obeyed, but she still hesitated. Finally, without another word, her haze gathered, and she took 1337's hand, disappearing with him into it.

Plungerman turned back to the others, raising one

of the grenades. *We've still got a job to do.* He pointed down the corridor, gesturing with the explosive, giving instructions. They'd managed to destroy the machine and the computers that controlled it, but they couldn't risk doing this halfway. If there was more data from the Toilet's experiments stored within the base, they had to do everything they could to make sure as little of it survived as possible.

Go, he signaled.

Most of his comrades obeyed, but a Speakerwoman—the one he'd bumped into earlier—lingered, waiting for him to follow.

Plungerman shook his head, directing her after the others. *I'll meet you outside. Go!*

This time, the Speakerwoman listened, though it was clear she didn't want to. But there was still something Plungerman needed to do, and he wasn't willing to involve any of the others, given how risky it was going to be. He turned the other way down the corridor, moving quickly through the hallways, anticipating at every moment that he'd run into a group of the enemy. Part of what he was counting on was that the Toilets would focus on pursuing the larger group of escapees; he didn't relish using them as semi-bait, but it also wasn't as if they were pushovers. If they stuck together, he had faith that they'd be able to escape from the facility and reunite with TV Woman and 1337 on the outside.

Plungerman reached a stairwell. Going up tugged at him, promising a chance to escape, but that wasn't his focus at the moment. He went down instead, tracing his route as best he could from his memory of the map they'd encountered earlier. He'd seen something on it, something that hadn't been important at the time but now would be exactly what they needed to pull off the crazy plan he had in mind.

As he descended the stairs, the vibration they'd felt all the way up on the surface became stronger, an indication that he was headed in the right direction. A facility like this needed more than a few smart Toilets and captured lab rats to keep it running—it also needed power. A lot of it. Which meant that there had to be a generator room, and if he'd interpreted the Skibidi map correctly, he should be getting close to it very soon. Finally he reached a lower level, the corridors here less well lit than above, with an emptier feeling. But the vibration was stronger than ever, and a chamber was visible at the end of the very long corridor in which he found himself. Plungerman bolted down it, unwilling to waste another moment. This needed to get done as fast as possible, before he could be discovered. Hopefully the others would have enough time to do what they needed to do to escape, but he couldn't wait on that.

The corridor spilled out into a long room with sickly yellow lighting.

Jackpot. Along one wall ran a line of generators. Even better, along the other were the hundreds of drums of fuel to feed those generators. That was exactly what he'd hoped to . . .

Something collided with him, knocking Plungerman to the ground. Suddenly he was on his back, teeth snapping at him as an oil-smudged Toilet—that had seemingly come out of nowhere—attacked, vicious as a rabid dog. Plunger held up an arm, stiffening with pain as the teeth clamped down, but he pushed back and rolled as they did, shoving the attacker off him, then kicked at the concrete floor to put some space between them. The Toilet recovered quickly though, and—bad news—it wasn't alone. Five more, all of various sizes and stained with soot and grease, converged on him. Plungerman reached for his weapons, forgetting that one had been lost back in the testing room and the other shredded to bits by the sonic attack.

It didn't matter. He still had his fists, and the . . .

He reached into his coat pockets, but they were empty. In the struggle, the grenades had been knocked free. He spotted them lying a few meters away, beyond the line of Toilets closing in on him.

Fists it was, then.

Plungerman jumped to his feet, dodging the first Toilet that lunged at him, grabbing it by the hair and twisting its face around before smashing it into its own tank, over and over again. It was only when another Toilet reached him that he yanked the flusher, finishing it off so that he could handle the next attack. No, two attackers this time—they snapped at him, one brandishing a jointed metal limb with a screwdriver at the end of it. It stabbed out, quick as lightning. Plunger barely avoided the strike, but it had been a feint, meant to send him into the attack range of its partner. Again he felt the sting of the alien's bite, this time to one leg, the teeth sinking deep. But in doing so, the Toilet had exposed its flusher. Plungerman struggled to get a grip as the Toilet shook him, but finally managed to close his fingers over it. He'd barely stumbled away from the flushed foe before another assault came: the stabbing screwdriver again, followed by the largest of the

Toilets, not big enough to be called Giant but easily towering a meter above Plungerman.

He grabbed the metal limb while dodging it yet again, with both hands, and managed to snap it off. The Toilet screeched with anger, but Plungerman simply turned the weapon on its former owner, thrusting it at the twisted features before shoving the critically injured Toilet at its massive friend. That only slowed the larger Toilet down for a moment. It continued lurching toward Plungerman, forcing him back until something impeded his progress. He risked a glance around: the fuel drums. There was no time to think—to consider what a terrible idea this was—only to stab. He plunged the screwdriver into one of the piled containers, guessing as best as he could at the height, anticipating that the whole thing would spark and blow them all to unidentifiable bits. Which, at least, would accomplish what he'd set out to do.

But luck hadn't finished with him quite yet. When he pulled the tool free, greenish liquid sprayed forth, directly into the large Toilet's face. It screamed, blinded by the caustic fluid, and stumbled backward, tripping over the last of its companions in the process. Taking advantage of the opening, Plungerman sprinted around the large Toilet and went for the smaller one.

As he did, pain shot up his side, and his leg went out. He went sprawling, expecting to see another attacker, one he'd somehow missed, but then he understood: The Toilet that had bitten him did some real damage, which he'd managed to exacerbate. One leg moved when he wanted; the other had gone completely dead. There was no time to figure out any other impairments, though—the smaller Toilet was on top of him within moments. Plungerman stabbed, the point of the screwdriver finding nothing but impenetrable metal, his injured arm failing to push the attacker off him. Desperate, he rolled, using all of his strength to send the Toilet to one side. Not expecting this, the Toilet collided with the concrete floor, stunned long enough for Plungerman to stab the screwdriver into one ear, so hard that its bloodied point appeared out the other side of the creature's head. It went stiff, eyes empty, before Plunger grabbed the flusher and finished it off.

Then he lay on the concrete, now stained with red. So close . . . He just needed to gather his strength a little longer . . .

Get up, he told himself. *Get up and finish what you started.*

Plungerman pushed himself up into a sitting

position. The large Toilet was stomping about still, blinded and angry about it, but Plunger's attention was on the grenades, and where they'd rolled. Five, he counted, one for each of the last Toilets he'd encountered in this horrible place. He tried to stand up, but with a dead leg, it wasn't happening. Instead, using his good arm, Plungerman pulled himself across the floor of the generator room until he reached the explosives. Two he rolled over to the wall of fuel drums. Two he tossed so that they were under the generators. If the others had done what he'd instructed, they'd be planting the remaining grenades throughout the facility as they fled, and once Plungerman triggered this set . . . Well, the chain reaction would do the rest, making sure the work the Toilets were doing here was utterly and completely wiped out.

Only one step left. He raised the final grenade, eyeing the pin. This hadn't been the plan. One to set the rest off, yes, but he'd pictured doing that from the floor of the hangar above, then running like hell. Well, best laid plans, and all that. He certainly wasn't going to be making any runs for it now or be clearing the facility before it exploded behind him, taking out all the Toilets still within and . . .

Titan Speakerman.

In all the commotion and fighting, he'd completely forgotten about their original goal of tracking the Titan. Was he still sedated and wired up, above? Would the explosions reach him too? Thinking back to what he'd seen earlier, Plunger could almost consider that the best outcome, as devastating as it would be. Or maybe the titan would feel the destruction coming and throw off his sedated stupor in time to avoid it. Would the survivors be able to avoid *him*, if any surviving Toilets turned the still-infected behemoth on the escaping Alliance fighters?

That Plungerman would never know was regrettable. But 1337 and TV Woman—admittedly he might have misjudged her a little—would deal with the situation; he had to believe that. They'd make sure as many of the freed captives got away as possible and that the Alliance would be informed of what occurred here.

Suddenly the large Toilet turned. Its eyes were shot with red—the normal kind, at least—and the skin around them burned from contact with the fuel, but it seemed to be able to see again. At least enough to zero in on him, now basically as helpless as they came.

It lurched toward Plunger, massive head stretching on its rubbery neck, growling so hard that little bits of spittle gathered at the edges of its mouth.

Oh, it was mad. And it was looking for some revenge.

Too bad it wasn't going to get it.

Plungerman looped one finger into the pin of the grenade.

Then he saw smoke. At first, he thought it must be a fire, that something had set off the damaged fuel drum, igniting the liquid that was still spilling out on the concrete floor. But no . . . there was something familiar about this smoke.

Because it wasn't smoke.

TV Woman appeared, crouching down beside him.

:3 appeared on her monitor. ".*pleh ym dedeen uoy taht uoy dloT ?eeS*"

Plungerman raised a finger at her. It wasn't a thumbs-up.

Her display changed. XD

Then Plungerman pulled the pin, lobbing the grenade toward the incoming, furious Toilet. It bounced off the grease-stained creature, then went . . .

Plungerman didn't see where. TV Woman grabbed him as the black cloud enveloped them both. The next thing he knew, cool, fresh air was hitting him in the face. It was still hazy, but the hazy gray light of incoming dawn, night beginning to fade from the cloud-speckled sky. Something else was there too, something large and moving quickly. TV Woman's boots crunched on the dirt beside him, and beyond those, Plungerman spotted another familiar figure: 1337. He was sitting on a patch of grass; they were on the same hill, Plunger realized, as when they'd arrived only hours before. 1337 had managed a rough bandage over his wounded knee, and there was a patch on his head, where the sparks had been spitting earlier. He nodded at Plungerman, giving him a thumbs-up before turning back to the valley below and the shape moving away from it, almost impossible to make out now.

Titan Speakerman. The Researcher Toilets working on him must have finally realized something bad was happening and sent him away. As much as he'd considered that the Titan's destruction might be a blessing, Plungerman found that he was relieved that their mind-controlled ally had escaped. That meant there was still a chance to remove the parasite, to free him and add his might back to the Alliance forces.

It was at that moment that the rumbling began. It reached them all the way up in the hills, which was how he knew that this new mission—not the one they'd set out on, but the one that needed to be accomplished—had been successful. Even better, he spotted a number of humanoid figures below, beyond where the former airstrip's asphalt ended, all jumping up and down. They could feel the rumbling too.

A moment later, one side of the hangar exploded. It was quickly followed by another burst of flame, and another, spreading until the entire airfield was engulfed, great clouds of smoke billowing into the sky. With nothing and no one to stop it, it would keep burning until all that was left of the Skibidi Toilet facility was scorched metal and ash.

Oh, a few tiny white figures did emerge, soot-darkened and frantic, but their former captives made short work of them—a satisfying task, Plungerman was sure.

Standing above him, TV Woman put her hands on her hips, her meaning clear. Victorious or not, they were still stuck in the middle of the desert. *".emoh edir a sgniht roop uoy teg retteB"*

But Plungerman held up a hand. *Wait.* Then he gestured at the line of pale yellow just beginning to peek over the distant horizon. It was a solid night's work that they'd done, a crippling blow that was one of many they'd struck—and would still need to strike—during this escalating war, but at this exact moment, they weren't in a rush. They didn't need to fight. And peace was not a luxury they experienced often.

Might as well take advantage of the rare opportunity, then, and spend a few minutes to watch the sun rise.

PART 3:

ENEMY OF MY ENEMY

Earth is overrun, no corner of the planet left untouched by the Skibidi Toilet invasion, which has only increased in intensity with the arrival of the Astro Toilets. Alliance forces are flung far and wide trying to mitigate this increasingly deadly threat, but successes remain elusive. As they seek new ways to resist, help arrives from the unlikeliest of places . . .

ONCE UPON A TIME, THEY CALLED THIS PLACE THE City of Light.

So much for *that*, thought Redd, crouched in a dark so complete that it was like being surrounded by an infinite void. The only break from it came via the occasional sweep of searchlights as they poured through the cracked walls of ruins where he and the remains of his squad were hidden. These brief illuminations offered glimpses of flaked gold gilding, chipped ornamentation, and expansive, formerly vibrant paintings that were now faded and spotted with mold—visions of lost magnificence, there and gone in seconds. At one time, this building must have been amazing to behold. But now, well into the Skibidi Toilet invasion, what was left of it was a mangled shell, the most amazing thing about it that it was still standing.

Another sweep came, spears of light poking through the countless holes in the walls, reaching deep into the interior of the structure. Thankfully the searchlights didn't slow, but they did offer Redd a chance to check on his squad members, tucked into a nearby corner as they hid among the piles of debris. Three—that's all that was left, a fact that hit him nearly as hard as the ambush had earlier. Though they'd been aware that the city was heavily infested with Skibidi Toilets, that initial explosion caught them off guard, seeming to come out of nowhere and instantly cutting the squad's number in half. The bomb had also left Redd's shoulder riddled with shrapnel damage. He lifted it, inspecting what he could as the last of the lights passed over. The cuts and punctures weren't life-threatening, but they were deep, and though Redd's hand and fingers still worked, his grip was weak. Not exactly helpful, though with some effort he could still muster the strength to pull a trigger.

Redd cradled his laser rifle close with his uninjured arm, knowing that they couldn't remain where they were much longer. The patrols had steadily increased in frequency; the Toilets knew they'd cornered their prey and were just narrowing down the places where they were hiding. If he didn't order the squad to make a move soon, they'd end up cornered here with little chance at retreat and no chance at overcoming the enemy's strength. Redd tightened as he cursed every last one of the alien Skibidi Toilet invaders. This reconnaissance assignment had gone bad in a way he'd never expected. Maybe . . . maybe he was getting complacent. Sloppy, even. Not long ago, the war seemed to have tipped in the Alliance's favor. The Siege of Alpha-Hills, despite the intensity of the fighting and the losses suffered, was considered a victory.

But there had been no reduction in the fighting since then; conversely it had actually intensified, mainly for one impossible-to-ignore reason: the Astro Toilets. The normal Skibidi Toilet aliens had been bad enough, but as more and more of the enhanced variants joined the war, the less it seemed the Alliance had the strength to come out victorious. It was the Astro Toilets who had Redd's squad cornered now. Their forces had pursued the squad through the city for a full day, picking off members one or two at a time. It was almost like the Astro Toilets were enjoying the hunt, playing a game with Redd's team. Well, it was going to be game over very soon if he didn't manage to find a way to get the rest of the squad out of the city and back into the relative safety of Alliance territory.

Overhead, the sounds of the Astro Toilet infantry, with their heavily armored toilet bodies and levitators that granted them flight, came again. This time, Redd took advantage of their searchlights, using them as a cover to signal his squad with the tiny handheld flashlight he carried. Three flashes in quick succession. *Get ready to move.* A Cameraman in a now tattered trench coat—the newest addition to Redd's squad—gave him a thumbs-up right before the darkness descended again. For a moment, Redd couldn't help but remember that day—long ago now—when *he'd* been the new recruit, hiding in the shadows on a mission that had similarly gone wrong. Too much time had passed since then, too much war and too many fallen comrades. It was nearly enough to make him want to remain where he was and be done with the seemingly endless battles.

Nearly, but not quite. *Get moving,* he told himself, pushing away the gray weight of losing so much of his squad. *You don't get to give up—not now, not tomorrow, not even if and when that final moment comes and you're staring down a situation there's no way out of.* Redd knew how they would win this war—not the exact way, but a more universal one that each and every member of the Alliance tried to take to heart: that to free Earth from the Toilet menace, they would have to keep fighting.

As the overhead patrols moved away, Redd clicked the flashlight back on. It was a calculated risk, but there was little chance they could navigate out of here in the dense dark. They would have to hope that the glow was weak enough that it wouldn't be spotted within the ruins of the building. The others were already on their feet. Redd signaled with a series of gestures—*stay close, stay quiet, hide if the patrols come again*—then got moving, leading them across the chamber and through the remains of what used to be a pair of huge ornate doors. Cautiously they wove through the scattered debris, taking care not to disturb any of it, lest the smallest sound give them away. This meant slow going as they wound their way around the edge of what used to be a grand hall until they reached the top of a wide marble staircase. Like the rest of the building, it must have been a majestic feature before being reduced to a pockmarked, half-demolished series of grime-coated steps.

At the bottom of these stairs, Redd spotted the building's foyer, still mostly intact despite a large hole where the main doors must have been. He pointed. *That's the way out.* Behind him, his three remaining squad members nodded, bracing themselves for when Redd clicked the flashlight off a moment later. It was too dangerous from here on out. They'd have to depend on the abstract, slightly less dark outline of the opening ahead to lead the way. Redd took point, moving slowly but deliberately across the hall, down another set of steps, and through the vestibule, all the while anticipating the reappearance of the Astro Toilets. But they reached the exit hole without incident, and though Redd held them there for several tense minutes, no more patrols appeared.

Redd was stationed on one side of the hole. On the other was the new recruit, who leaned out as far as he dared as he scanned the empty sky above. Then he shrugged at Redd, no doubt wondering the same thing as his leader. Had the Astro Toilets given up? Were they concentrating on another part of the ruined city, doing more careful inspections as they tried to flush their prey? Either explanation was one more reason that they needed to get out of here fast and not give the Astros the opportunity to corner the squad again.

Redd signaled once more. Beyond their egress was an open space: the remains of a plaza that sat at the juncture of several streets. At the plaza's center was an entrance to the old subway. That's where they were headed. Another gamble—many of the tunnels were at least partially caved in—but given the increased Astro Toilet presence on the surface, it was worth the risk. With a little bit of luck, the old metro lines could lead them into a far less infested section of the city, where they could resurface and make a real escape.

After one last search of the night skies, Redd counted down with his fingers: *Three . . . two . . . one . . .*

Silent as shadows, the remains of the squad crept forward. Redd stayed in the lead but signaled for the new recruit to take up the rear. He rushed to obey, gripping his laser rifle like they were stranded in the middle of the ocean and the weapon were a life preserver. Not that the rifles were particularly effective against the Astro Toilets. Redd sorely wished that they'd come more heavily armed, with rocket launchers, or at least a few grenades. Hindsight was 20/20 though; add it to the list of regrets he'd had over the last twenty-four hours.

Twenty meters to the subway entrance . . . ten . . .

They were only steps away when the sky exploded with lights, a trio of forms zipping into sight at a speed impossible for any creature of earthly origin. But not for the Astro Toilets—within seconds, the ugly, helmeted faces of the enemy were grinning down, pleased in a way that told Redd that the enemy had been looking forward to this.

Go! Redd took off at a run as he tried to close the remaining distance to the subway. There was one advantage left to them: The tunnels wouldn't allow easy access for the large, bulky Astros. If the squad could just get underground, maneuver into some narrow space that offered them passage but impeded the Astros' pursuit, maybe they could still—

The street in front of them suddenly exploded, sending Redd careening through the air. He collided with the street, rolling to an abrupt stop on his back. Stunned, he lay there for some indeterminate amount of time, feeling as if he'd hit every cobblestone left in the plaza, trying to get his bearings back. Where were the Astro Toilets? Where was the rest of his squad? A face appeared above him—the new recruit. His camera's carapace was dented and he was covered in dust, but he was alive. Grabbing Redd's arm, the new recruit pulled him back onto his feet as Redd fought to shake off the effects of the impact. The others—had they managed to . . .

He stopped. Nearby, two figures lay sprawled beneath chunks of stone and concrete, deathly still.

Laughter sounded from above. The Astro Toilets were relishing in their victory, playing with the remains of their quarry like the way a cat toys with a mouse before finally consuming it. Rage filled Redd, enough to make him push through the pain, through the damage. He shoved the new recruit aside, then grabbed his laser rifle from where it had landed and began firing at the hovering enemy. The Astro Toilets were overconfident, so assured the squad was beaten that they didn't expect the attack. Redd's shots hit one of the Toilets, not enough to punch through its enhanced armor, but enough to knock it off balance and send it spiraling through the air while the others scattered.

That bought a few seconds. The subway was out of the question—the entrance was completely blocked by rubble now—so they ran instead, heading for one of the many side streets that ran off the plaza. What other choice was there? At least in the labyrinthine ruins of the city, a lone pair of Cameramen might have the chance to elude the Astro Toilets again. Running as fast as their battered bodies would carry them, Redd and the recruit darted down the nearest avenue, turning off it almost immediately as they plunged into a twisted alley, then cut through a hole in the cityscape where a now demolished building once stood. On the other side of that, Redd spotted a covered passage.

He pointed. *There!*

Within the passage, their movements would be hidden from the Astro Toilets, who had regathered themselves and were in pursuit again. The new recruit nodded, shoving Redd ahead of him before turning to lay down cover fire on the advancing enemy. Redd reached the passage, getting a few steps under cover before raising his own weapon, ready to return the favor.

It was just in time to see the closest Astro Toilet fire its own lasers, a volley that caught the now running new recruit square in the back. The momentum of the blow carried him the last few steps and directly into Redd's arms. He dragged the injured Cameraman deeper under cover, then laid the new recruit down, pulling his trench coat aside to assess how much damage there was . . .

Even as he did it, Redd knew it was already too late. The last member of his squad—and its newest—never even saw what hit him.

That was it.

Redd was the last one left standing.

Again the desire to give up sparked and began to burn him from the inside. He'd failed to save the recruit, failed to save *any* of them. The entirety of his squad had now joined the long list of Alliance dead who would never get a chance to see the other side of war, or witness the final defeat of the Toilets. As Redd stared down at the recruit's body though, cold anger rose like a flash flood, pouring over the despair and extinguishing it. Giving up now would render his squad's sacrifice pointless and unacknowledged. But if he kept running, made it out of the city alive . . .

Redd spent a few more seconds mourning the lost charge at his feet and then turned, taking off down the corridor. And not a moment too soon. Behind him, he could hear one of the Astro Toilets attempting to enter the passageway, but from the frustrated sounds that followed, it was clear they wouldn't fit.

Good. Redd took one turn and then another. The passage didn't last long; after another dozen meters, it dumped him into a courtyard tucked between buildings. He checked the square of sky above, and it was clear, so he darted through it, passing into an entrance archway and slipping between the half-destroyed metal gates there. That brought him onto another street. The Astro Toilets were nowhere to be seen. Directly in front of him, across the avenue, another alleyway waited, narrow enough to provide him some cover. Redd dashed toward it, cringing at the sound of his footsteps on the stone, hoping they didn't give him away. Fortunately the alley's high walls seemed to dampen the noise once he'd reached it. The passage was almost perfectly straight, narrow and dim before it bent abruptly at a hard right angle.

Redd took the turn and froze.

Directly ahead of him stood a Skibidi Toilet. Not one of his Astro Toilet pursuers, but rather a different sort of advanced variant—a Mutant. This one was nearly entirely human in its appearance, if you didn't count the misshapen proportions and the spinning saw blade at the end of one arm appendage. Despite the fact that it was nighttime, the Mutant wore sunglasses, and it grinned at him with a wicked, bony smile, clearly pleased at having intercepted Redd's escape. Redd spun, attempting to go back the way he'd come, but it was too late. Behind him, an equally ecstatic Astro Toilet had appeared, just beyond the alley opening. It was a tight fit, but the creature was able to enter, advancing slowly as the other two Astro Toilets appeared on the rooftop above, faces beaming with as much intensity as their searchlights, which pinned Redd in place.

He was trapped. Redd looked around—for a window, for a door, anything that might offer an escape, but his luck had run out. There was nowhere else to run. This was it; his squad was dead, and soon he would be too. How long before his superiors figured out they weren't coming back and carried the news of his demise to those in the Alliance he called friends? That was the only question that was left to ask, a consideration quickly followed by the last decision Redd would ever make: that if he was going down, he was going to go down fighting.

Backed into a corner both literally and figuratively, Redd raised his laser rifle. The encroaching Astro Toilet was on one side of him, the Buzzsaw Mutant on the other, its blade spinning menacingly. He wasn't sure which to fire on first, but during the instant he hesitated, the decision was made for him: The Astro Toilet in the alleyway suddenly surged forward, fast as lightning. Redd began to fire, but he was immediately knocked into the wall. A dark form filled his view even as he heard the sharp scream of metal against metal. A moment later, something dark and wet splattered against the brick beside him.

Blood.

The whirring, shrieking sound stopped. Redd looked up. At first he didn't understand what he was seeing. Limned by the searchlights, the Buzzsaw Mutant loomed over both him and the now very dead Astro Toilet. That didn't make any sense though. Had the sunglasses obstructed the Mutant's vision, made him think he was attacking Redd as he accidentally struck the Astro Toilet instead?

There was no chance to sort it out. Enraged by the loss of one of their own, the Astro Toilets on the roof screeched and reared into the air, weapons taking aim. But before they could fire, one of the Astro Toilets bucked suddenly, struck by a volley of intense laser blasts from an unseen source. The second Astro Toilet turned to help, but a dark figure collided with it, pulling it down and out of view. Redd had no idea what was happening, but instinct took over: An enemy was right in front of him, and he needed to take it down fast. He raised his rifle.

Seeing this, the Mutant suddenly backed off, throwing its hands into the air. "Wait!"

Redd's finger froze against the trigger. He knew he should follow through—this was a *Skibidi Mutant,* as dangerous and deadly as any of the other invaders—but something wasn't adding up. Logic wrestled with his gut, and for the moment, his gut was coming out on top.

A moment later, the body of an Astro Toilet crashed down into the space between him and the Mutant. Redd threw up an arm to protect himself from the brief burst of flames, but it wasn't even enough to singe the arm of his overcoat. The Buzzsaw Mutant was unharmed as well, and was looking up at where the fallen foe had come from. More confused than ever, Redd followed its gaze. Above, the last of the Astro Toilets that had pursued him was dead as well, slumped over the edge of the roof. Another Skibidi Mutant—female this time, helmeted and heavily armored—stood over that corpse. But it was the trio to one side of the Mutant that finally made Redd wonder whether he'd taken a hit to the head without realizing it. Surely he had to be malfunctioning.

One of the figures was a Cameraman wearing a military beret and a long trench coat. Beside him stood a Speakerman, taller than the Cameraman even without the ten-gallon hat perched atop his speaker head. And the third . . .

Redd's chest tightened as she moved into the light still emanating from the Astro Toilet's corpse. He already knew that silhouette, could recognize it from a mile away, no matter how dark the night.

Zero.

The Camerawoman stepped one foot up onto the edge of the building and raised a hand, giving him a little wave, as if they'd run into each other in some Alliance base and not in the midst of one of the most Toilet-infested cities on this continent.

The moment turned surreal. It seemed impossible, but there she was, her lens glinting at him in that oh-so-familiar way. Redd hadn't seen his former commander-turned-friend in . . . Well, it had been a while. Zero's squad had been the first one he ever served in, but the needs of the war had eventually seen Redd reassigned, and then given his own squad to command. They'd crossed paths from time to time, fought alongside each other in battles, even shared command of a combined force once during a particularly large offensive. But even that had been ages ago. And now, when luck or fate or whatever had brought them back together, why had it done so in the company of two Skibidi Mutants, their enemies?

Redd took a confused step back, hitting the wall behind him. The Buzzsaw Mutant merely watched, waiting patiently as the others scaled carefully down the side of the building to street level. When they had reached it, Redd wasted no time demanding answers. He jabbed a finger at the Mutants. *What is going on? What are you doing with them?*

Zero moved carefully toward Redd, as if afraid to spook him, hands raised placatingly. *I can explain.* She nodded at his rifle. *Mind pointing that somewhere else though?*

Redd hadn't even realized he'd raised the weapon again. He felt like he was spinning, the confusion about what he was seeing overwhelming his senses in a way even the heat of battle rarely did. But he shook his head.

Zero seemed to read his mind. She turned, slowly, so that her neck was visible. On one of their first missions, Redd had been taken over by a Skibidi Toilet parasite, operated like a puppet until the damage it had sustained caused its control to falter and allow Redd brief periods of autonomy again. He'd managed to broadcast intel to the Alliance, had played a major part in helping them develop the technology that led to freeing the infected from their parasites. Zero knew that, knew that he'd be thinking something similar must have happened. But her neck was clear.

Letting the gun drop, though not releasing it, Redd raised one hand to his head, trying to chase the muddled sensation away. His injured arm moved slowly, barely obeying. Seeing this, Zero rushed over. *You're hurt!* She beckoned the Speakerman over. Still stunned, Redd could only stare at the Speakerman's flashy hat as he began inspecting Redd and pulling tools from his belt, poking and prodding the damage with practiced movements. The medical attention wasn't unwelcome, but explanations were a bigger priority. Redd pulled away, gesturing again angrily at the two Mutants.

The Speakerman made a twangy but pacifying noise, then pointed at himself. *"Name's Techs."* His metallic voice was surprisingly melodious. He then pointed at the other Cameraman—*"Sergeant"*—and finally the Mutants: *"Buzz. Sis."*

"Good to meet you, buddy," said Buzz, grinning intensely.

"Sorry about your team." Sis actually sounded sincere. "You clearly put up a good fight."

Redd nodded, despite the fact that the introductions

didn't clear up in the least why they were fighting alongside the Alliance. But Sergeant tipped his head knowingly as Techs went back to working on Redd's arm. *Yeah, it looks weird, right?*

His confident air cleared one thing up at least: who was in charge of this bizarre operation. Sergeant waved at Sis, who stepped forward. For the first time, Redd noticed the bulky sack she carried, slung over one shoulder. Whatever was in it remained a mystery as she raised one arm, where a panel lit up. Suddenly a small projection of G-Toilet appeared, perfectly rendered down to his needle-sharp stare. The leader of the Skibidi Toilets had a serious, grim look on his face. *"Hello,"* the projection said, before continuing in the Skibidi language. Redd didn't know exactly what was being said, but a general understanding began to grow as the projection shifted to familiar recordings, ones that showed G-Toilet clashing with Overseer Astro Toilet and Detainer Astro Toilet, leaders of the Astro faction. Not long ago, it had seemed G-Toilet was dead, only for the truth to come out later: that the G-Toilet killed by the two elite Astro Toilets was actually a decoy.

The projection cut off. Sis lowered her arm and said, "We have a common enemy."

Buzz gave one of the Astro Toilet bodies an angry kick. "Friends now, yeah?"

Redd could only stare. He heard the words, but it took a few moments to make sure that he'd understood them correctly. Then he turned to Sergeant, imploring him. *Are we really considering teaming up with them?*

Sergeant simply shrugged, unconcerned. *Not my call, but looks like yes.*

Still, it wasn't until Zero crossed her arms, in that way she did when she was extra serious, that Redd fully understood what was being communicated to him. That as impossible as it seemed, the Alliance and the Skibidi Toilets were now considering allying against the bigger threat: the Astro Toilets. It aligned with some of the vague intel he'd heard lately—about the overthrowing of G-Toilet's leadership and the death of Chief Scientist Skibidi Toilet. Something in the war was shifting, had been for a while.

Redd tensed. No, this was wrong. After how long they'd spent fighting the Skibidi Toilets . . . now they were simply going to join up with them? *Trust* the creatures that had been their sworn enemies up until now? It was crazy.

Then again, so was the rescue that had just taken place.

Techs finished his fiddling, making one last adjustment. Suddenly Redd could move his arm again, unimpeded. He flexed his fingers open and shut, working out the lingering stiffness.

Techs gave him a thumbs-up. *My work here is done.*

Redd didn't know what to do. He looked at the Mutants again, then down at his repaired arm, and finally at the rifle he held, hanging at his side.

Zero placed a placating hand on Redd's shoulder and stared at him intently. *I know what this looks like,* the gesture said. *And how unbelievable it seems. But you need to trust me.*

He did. It was about the only thing keeping Redd from using his laser rifle to take out some confused frustration on the nearby Mutants, allies or not. Sergeant, Techs... He didn't know them. But Zero... Of all the members of the Alliance, she was one of the few he'd put his faith in without question.

Redd's shoulders slumped. *Okay.* But accepting the situation wasn't the full measure of the explanation he needed. He looked around questioningly. *What happened?*

Zero tipped her chin at Sis, who let the sack she

was carrying drop open, though gingerly, as if protective of its contents. Inside was a TV Man—the head of one, anyway. As Redd watched, the head took off, levitating out of the bag until it hovered a few feet above the pavement. There, the TV Man wavered back and forth, swaying in a perplexing fashion as expressions flashed in rapid fire across his cracked screen.

@_@

:D

>o<

:3

Zero pointed at the dead Astro Toilets, telling Redd who'd inflicted the damage that had left the TV Man in this state.

But it was Sis who added the last piece of the puzzle. "We called a truce . . . have a message to deliver. But our meetup . . . went wrong. Your comrade got the worst of it."

Sergeant waved an irritated hand. *So much for our exit strategy.*

Redd had seen the TV Men disengage their heads before in order to attack the enemy, but he'd never encountered a situation where a head remained unattached from its body, which he assumed had been abandoned somewhere, damaged beyond repair. And apparently without it, the TV Man's teleportation powers were useless.

"So . . . Plan B," Buzz explained. "We head for the extraction point." He raised his buzz saw and let it whir briefly, grinning even wider than before. "Who likes things easy anyway?"

Zero nodded again, confirming what had been said. But it didn't make Redd feel any better. In fact, it made him feel worse. His squad had been sent into the city with standard, if vague, instructions: Sweep for the enemy, report back on their positions. Had they unwittingly been part of this plan? Had Redd's squad, as well as others, been used as a distraction in order to allow this clandestine meeting to take place?

On one hand, it made sense that they would want to get these supposed new allies and their message to Alliance territory as soon as possible. On the other hand, it seemed convenient that their TV Person—the member of the team who was able to teleport them to safety—was the only one who'd taken significant damage. What if that had been intentional? A TV Person, even their head alone, would be a big prize for the Skibidi invaders. They'd already tried re-creating the TV abilities at least once before; maybe they were still hoping to make some progress on that front. The defection of the Skibidi Toilets could be a cover to lure the Alliance in and make them let down their guard.

But if so, why were the Mutants still working alongside Zero and the others?

Sergeant clapped his hands. *Can't stand around here all day, kids.* He looked to Zero. *Your friend coming along?*

Redd took a few decisive, if shaky, steps forward. *Yes, I'm coming.* He didn't trust the Mutants, not in the least. This had to be a trick. And if it was, the last thing he was going to do was let them get away with it without paying for what had happened to his squad.

Not to mention he wasn't about to leave Zero alone with them.

Soon they were back on the move, leaving the alley behind and falling into a common Alliance formation, slightly off-kilter thanks to the addition of the two Mutants. They walked at the center of the pack, trailing Sergeant and Techs, the scrambled TV Man's head stowed away again in the bag. Following them were Zero and Redd, an arrangement that felt strangely familiar. How many other times had he and Zero walked at each other's side while on patrol? Thankfully there was no sign of any other Astro Toilets nearby at the moment, though Redd used his apprehension of their reappearance as an excuse to keep his guard up around the Mutants.

Zero remained vigilant as well, though Redd felt her attention repeatedly falling on him, scrutinizing as if he was still part of her crew, and not an Alliance leader in his own right these days.

Eventually he threw her a thumbs-up. *I'm okay, really.*

She nodded. *I know.* Still, she looked unsure. *It's only that . . .*

He waved a hand, knowing where her concern was stemming from. *Yeah. I get it.*

He'd lost his entire squad. There was no way she was going to let that go unacknowledged. Zero knew the pain of that experience, having lost more of her charges during the war than she could probably remember.

Redd pointed at her, trying to change the subject. *You . . .* He looked away, nervous. *It's been a while. You look good.*

Zero tossed her head in what was her equivalent of a laugh, then tipped her head at his stained and singed coat. *You look terrible.*

Redd couldn't help but share her amusement. Then he traced a circle in front of his lens before pointing a finger up from his camera head, as if something pointy had sprouted there. *You seen Spike lately?*

To his relief, Zero nodded. The Speakerman was the first of his kind Redd had ever met, initially saving Redd's life before becoming one of his closest friends. He waited for more, worrying a little as Zero hesitated, as if she wanted to say something but wasn't sure how.

Instead, she indicated all around them, following it with a thumbs-down. *Spike's not here, thankfully.* Then she made a series of hand signals, some of which indicated a particular Alliance base, following those by pointing at her own lens. *He's on a little break. Last I knew he was assigned to surveillance.*

Poor Spike, Redd couldn't help but think. His Speakerman friend preferred being in the middle of the action. He was probably bored to death with whatever feed-monitoring task the Alliance leaders had saddled him with.

Then again, it was a good thing Spike wasn't here. It was bad enough Zero was. The thought hit Redd like a fresh blow. It wasn't that Zero couldn't handle herself in a fight—heck, she'd probably wipe the floor with him, both the Mutants, and most of the Astros in the city if given half a chance—it was only that . . .

His head hung. Seeing his whole squad fall, one after the other . . . Redd felt the understanding bite deep, knowing he wouldn't be able to handle it right now if he had to watch the same thing happen to Zero too.

But it's not like they had a choice about the predicament they were in. Zero hadn't swooped in to rescue him; she'd been on her own mission. That her . . . well, her strange team came across him was nothing more than a stroke of good luck. For Redd, at least. He eyed the sack with the TV Man's head. If the teleporter hadn't been so badly damaged, Redd would be dead right now. But Zero would be somewhere else, likely in an Alliance base, safe and sound.

He wasn't sure which was the better outcome.

Sergeant signaled suddenly and they stopped. Then he waved toward a cracked wall and the courtyard visible beyond it. Silent, they all moved into the space, taking cover in the dark overgrown garden. A few tense minutes passed before Redd saw why: An Astro Toilet contingent flew by, brief glimpses of them visible as they buzzed by the cracked wall. They didn't slow, fortunately—probably a patrol that just happened to be passing through this area. Still,

Sergeant kept the squad where they were, making sure the enemy wouldn't loop around again.

In the meantime, he crept over to where Redd was hidden, taking the opportunity to expand on what "Plan B" meant. Using a stick, Sergeant traced lines in the hard-packed mud of the courtyard: first, two gently curving squiggles that ran nearly parallel to each other, followed by a pair of oval shapes with pointed ends within the gap between those two lines. Redd nodded his understanding. This was the river that ran through the city and the two islands that sat within it. Then Sergeant drew an X to the north of one bank—their approximate position. On the other side of the waterway, to the south and west, he drew a second X—the spot where they were to rendezvous for extraction.

It didn't seem far, but Redd knew the scale of the map was misleading. There was a lot of ground to cover, through a lot of what was undisputed Astro Toilet territory at the moment. Sergeant seemed to know this as well. He carefully drew another line from their position, through the city, until he reached the edge of the river. There he added a long, straight rectangle reaching from one shore to the other. That was a bridge, one of the few that still stood intact. A harrowing notion to say the least—there was little to no cover on the bridge. When they crossed, they'd be all but completely exposed to any Astro Toilets that might be nearby. But it wasn't like there were any other options.

Reaching into his pocket, Sergeant pulled out a device that looked a little like the small flashlights they carried, only with a small light on top and a button just below that. A beacon. Once they got to the rendezvous spot, Sergeant would trigger it, signaling to the Alliance to pick them up. Then he pointed up to the star-speckled sky above. The moon was just peeking over the edge of the building beside them, a white hornlike sliver looking as if it were growing out of the roof. *Best to do this under cover of dark.*

All around, they gave thumbs-up in agreement on that point. That didn't leave them much time though.

Assured that the Astro Toilets weren't coming back, they started to travel again, slinking through the streets as quickly as they dared, constantly on the lookout for any movement that might indicate the enemy. Every so often, when they reached a break in between the buildings or came out into a plaza at the center of the narrow, winding avenues, they spotted some

Astro Toilets in the distance, zipping through the air with their levitators. Whenever that happened, they'd duck behind cover and wait for the threat to disappear from sight.

After an hour or so of this, when Redd estimated that they must be getting close to the river, Buzz suddenly went on guard, staring off to their left down a side street. Redd, still in the rear of their party, froze as the Mutant spun his blade, the sound alerting Sergeant and Techs—and also, it seemed, whatever the Mutant had spotted. His distorted human face suddenly spun back toward Redd, sunglasses glinting in the moonlight.

"Run!" he yelled.

No. Redd remained where he was at first, sure it was a trick. But when Zero obeyed, he had to follow. The whole group took off, racing down the long avenue they had been traveling as Redd kept twisting around to see what had set Buzz off. But nothing appeared. He jabbed Zero in the upper arm to get her attention and pointed behind them. *There's nothing!*

Zero twisted her head around.

It's some kind of trick, Redd tried to communicate, starting to slow, but suddenly a dark shadow appeared, reflected by Zero's lens. This time, when he looked behind them, Redd saw something that turned him cold all over: Strider Astro Toilets. They were more earthbound than their fully airborne counterparts, but still able to levitate and move shockingly quick on their mechanical legs. There were half a dozen at least, maybe more, headed the team's way.

It was Zero's turn to give Redd a slap on the shoulder. *Faster!*

He didn't wait to be told twice, picking up the pace to close the gap that had opened up between them and the others. But the team came to a halt only moments later, so suddenly that Redd almost collided with the sack carrying the TV Man's head. There were more Strider Astro Toilets ahead.

"What now, new friends?" said Buzz as Sis raised her weapon, ready. "We can take them," she spat.

No! Sergeant shook his head, looked around frantically, then pointed at a high archway to their right. *There. We have to get through there.*

Easier said than done. A metal portcullis stretched across the archway, not so high that they couldn't climb it, but that wasn't going to happen before the Strider Astros reached them.

"Take this!" Sis shoved the sack at Redd, who

stumbled back under the unexpected weight. The bag's opening slipped to one side, revealing part of the TV Man's screen. Static flared there, followed by a confused ?????, but Redd covered it again and slung the sack over his shoulder, getting out of the way right before Sis began firing on the metal gate. Lucky for them, it was so rusted that her weapons cut through it like a knife through butter—a gap opened, just wide enough for them to pass through.

Sergeant and Techs slipped inside, Zero on their heels.

"Well," Sis spat at him over her shoulder, now firing at the oncoming Astros. "What are you waiting for?"

The trap, Redd thought. *Whatever it is that you're about to drop on us.* He'd been a captive of the Skibidi Toilets once before; there was no way he was going to go through that horror again.

But Buzz started shoving him at the opening as Sis continued to lay down cover fire. Reluctantly Redd obeyed, passing through the barrier into a tunnel that spilled out into a wide plaza. This was a mistake, he thought immediately. There was no cover here, save for a few piles of rubble left where the buildings surrounding them had taken damage. The structures formed a horseshoe shape around three sides of the sprawling plaza; on the fourth, a flat, withered park stretched into the distance, an option that was only good if they hoped to be surrounded almost immediately.

But maybe that's what the Mutants had planned all along.

Redd signaled frantically at Zero and Sergeant. *This has to be a trap! We're sitting ducks out here!*

Sergeant lolled his head back and waved dismissively. *Relax, would you? Always so worried.*

The Mutants finally caught up, accompanied by Techs. Redd hadn't seen the Speakerman as he passed through the arch, too distracted by an expected betrayal.

But the reason for Techs's brief delay became clear when he raised a detonator. "*Get ready!*" he said, and pressed a button.

Redd had barely enough time to duck and cover as a series of explosions rang out, as quick and sharp as popcorn popping. Then came a rumble. Only steps away, the archway collapsed, cutting off the entrance from the street.

"Not bad," said Buzz, grinning.

Techs noticed Redd's surprise. "*What?*" he rumbled, gesturing at Redd's repaired shoulder. "*You think that was the only reason I came along?"* From his pockets, he drew out a small metal disc about the size of a hockey puck and tossed it over.

Redd caught the explosive. It was vaguely familiar—something he'd used during some training session or other. Small, but it packed a punch when used correctly, as he'd just witnessed. They could be detonated remotely, like Techs had done, or set to go off with a built-in timer. A handy little item, when it came down to it.

Redd started to pass the bomb back, but Techs waved him away. *"Keep it."* Then he took the sack with the TV Man's head. *"I can carry this for a while."*

Redd started to object, but he stopped, preferring to have both hands free to operate his rifle. Especially given the Mutants' continued proximity. He eyed Buzz. Those Strider Astro Toilets seemed to come out of nowhere. Had the Mutant signaled them, either with his saw or in some other way, alerting the Striders to their location?

The Mutant caught Redd staring and held his gaze, as if in challenge. "Something you would like to say?"

Redd took a challenging step toward him.

Then Sergeant snapped his fingers. *Okay, wrap it up. We have to keep moving.*

Again Redd pointed at the coverless plaza and the park that could now be more accurately called a death trap. *Are you crazy?* The collapse of the archway would slow the Strider Astro Toilets down, but not for long. *Where are we supposed to go?*

Sergeant turned to Zero with exasperation. *Is he always like this?*

Zero shrugged noncommittally.

Sergeant slashed a hand at the plaza. *We aren't going that way.* He indicated the buildings around them instead. *We use those as cover, hide inside, and find another spot to exit where they won't see us.*

Redd had to admit it wasn't the worst idea. It also wasn't a good one. Within the buildings, they wouldn't even have the light of the moon to guide them through the dark. But options were in short supply. With another quick check of the skies, Sergeant got them moving, heading for a skeletal structure that sat near one end of the plaza. Not much of the crisscrossed metal framework remained, the ground around it littered with shards of glass, but within and below it, a new space opened up. As it turned out, Sergeant's plan wasn't so different than Redd's earlier one: head underground. This was no subway though; moving one by one, they carefully descended into a vast subterranean chamber. Sergeant flipped on his flashlight, gesturing for the others to do the same. The little handheld tools didn't do much, but the Mutants had shoulder-mounted lights, which they turned on as well. Suddenly Redd could see how truly large a space they'd found themselves in. Halls branched off from this central chamber, leading off into more darkness. The remains of a map, almost unreadable, hung on a wall nearby, enough left of it to give Redd the impression that they'd entered what could almost be considered a subterranean city in its own right.

Which way? Redd shrugged at Sergeant.

Their leader looked around, considering the options. It wasn't an easy question. Every branch looked as dark and uninviting as the others, and while they knew the general direction they wanted to be headed, the goal wasn't necessarily to come out close to the river, but rather where the Astro Toilets would be least likely to find them.

Buzz pointed up a set of crumbling stairs, at one of the hallways that seemed to have the least amount of damage and debris. "What about that way?"

Sergeant considered this, but Redd shook his head vehemently. *We can't take orders from them.* He pointed up to the skies and plaza above, still clear, but for who knew how long?

Sis scoffed. "If we wanted to betray you, there are easier ways."

Redd crossed his arms angrily. *Unless this is all part of your plan.*

"Do you not understand yet?" Sis frowned. "You are not the only ones taking a risk—"

Zero clapped her hands sharply. *Enough.* Then she headed for the hallway Buzz had indicated. Tight with frustration, Redd had no other choice but to fall in behind the others as they followed her lead. Including Sis, who rolled her eyes at him before doing so.

This was ridiculous. Anger gripped Redd as they made their way into tighter, narrower halls. They'd been fighting the Skibidi Toilets for how long? He'd personally watched Zero kill countless Toilets, with a vehemence that few others in the Alliance could match. She'd even earned her name from the fact that she never, if she could help it, left more than zero Skibidi Toilets alive. And now here she was, working with the enemy and expecting him to do the same without question. He wanted to trust her—he *did* trust her—but it was still madness.

Ahead, Sis had taken up position just behind Zero, helping to light the way, but Buzz was right in front of Redd. The Mutant's back was to him. He still had his rifle . . . it would be so easy. Just take aim and fire. No one could tell Redd that the Mutant didn't deserve it. How many Alliance members had he killed before this? Dozens? Hundreds? The Mutants were tough and deadly, as much a threat as the Astro Toilets. *Still* a threat, Redd was sure of it.

He thought about his squad, their bodies still scattered across the city where they'd fallen. Their newest recruit, who had all but died in Redd's arms, barely given a chance to fight in this war before he'd ended up scrapped. It wasn't fair—no, it wasn't *right* that after losing everyone that they had, Redd would be asked to set it all aside and team up with the monsters he'd known as enemies only hours ago. Who cared that they had a message for the Alliance leaders? It was from G-Toilet, another beast who deserved what the Astro Toilets had tried to do to him. Redd only regretted that they hadn't done a more thorough job and actually killed the Skibidi Toilet leader instead of one of his decoys.

The frustration was so deep and so gripping that Redd hardly noticed that he'd stopped moving, and that his finger had slipped behind the trigger of the weapon. A couple quick movements and it would be done, easy as so many other times he'd taken down the enemy.

Alerted by the cessation of Redd's footsteps, Buzz suddenly stopped. This caused the others to pause as well. They all turned and looked back at him.

"Something wrong?" Buzz's voice was questioning but guileless. For some reason, that enraged Redd even further. His grip tightened on his weapon, but then Zero was there, moving so that she stood between him and the Mutant.

She gave him an unsure thumbs-up. *Everything okay?*

Redd loosened. He nodded back down the hallway behind him. *Thought I heard something.* He released the trigger and returned the thumbs-up. *It was nothing. We're good.*

That was enough assurance for the team, who started walking again. All save for Zero. Instead of returning to her forward position, she fell in beside Redd and tipped her head, the small movement enough to communicate exactly what she was thinking. *You're not going to do something stupid are you?*

Redd gestured angrily. *Why shouldn't I?* He drew a

finger across his throat in a cutting motion. *We should be taking them down, not teaming up with them!*

Zero's shoulders fell a little, as if there was a part of her that didn't disagree. *I know.* Then she straightened, indicating Sergeant ahead. *We have our orders. We're going to follow them.*

Redd threw up his hands in exasperation. *Even if they are crazy?*

Zero nodded. *Yep.*

Had everyone lost their mind except him? Redd fought for control, his thoughts an increasingly frantic mess as he tried to figure out what the Skibidi Toilets' angle was. A TV Man head wasn't enough for the trouble the Mutants were going through, but they must be doing this on purpose, using this false overture of shared goals to infiltrate the Alliance, attack it from the inside somehow. What other explanation was there? The Skibidi Toilets didn't want to make friends; they wanted to take over the planet and be in total control. That couldn't have changed overnight.

Or could it have? There was no denying that the Astros were more dangerous than their predecessors, and that they'd managed to gain territory and damage the Alliance workings in countless devastating ways. But would the Skibidi Toilets turn on their own?

Redd steeled himself. *No.* Despite what the others thought, he refused to buy into the lie. He'd fought in this war long enough to know who the enemy was—Skibidi Toilet, Astro Toilet, it didn't matter. They all needed to go. But with Sergeant and Techs and Zero still convinced that the Mutants were allies, Redd would have to bide his time. Sooner or later the Mutants would turn on them, and when they did, he'd be ready.

They traveled slowly, room by room, until it began to feel like they were navigating a maze. But each chamber was more interesting than the last. As much devastation as had befallen the city, some of what surrounded them remained untouched by the war. They passed countless statues—humanoid, but with strange animal heads instead of normal ones. There were shelves full of pottery, fragments of stone walls, jewelry wrought in gold and silver and precious gems that glittered when their flashlights swept over the cases that held them. When Redd's foot hit something, he looked down to see a vibrant flash of blue. He picked it up, discovering a figurine of a rotund animal, which he placed carefully back on a shelf with some other figurines, all coated in a thick layer of dust.

The twists and turns continued, sometimes turning

into a short set of stairs, other times into long passages with no offshoots. Suddenly there was a commotion up ahead. Redd lifted the rifle, ready for an attack, but when Buzz moved to one side, he found Techs wrestling with the sack. The TV Man's head was apparently in a state of panic, trying to fly away. But hindered by the covering and Techs's arms wrapped around it, it couldn't get airborne.

"Whoa, whoa . . ." Techs was humming, trying to calm the TV Man. Finally he pulled the covering away. Sickly static filled the TV Man's screen, but more concerning were the sparks spitting from where his neck should have been. They rained down on the marble floors, looking briefly like stars in the sky before they winked out of existence. Sis came to Techs's rescue, her hands clamping down on either side of the boxy head, holding it steady.

Sergeant tipped his head questioningly. *What's wrong with him?*

Techs made an exasperated noise. "*What does it look like?*" But he waved a dismissive hand. "*I can handle it. Give me a few minutes.*"

Sergeant didn't look pleased, but he spun a finger in the air. *Okay. Let's take a rest.*

Redd didn't like the idea of stopping either, but

Zero didn't hesitate to find a spot to sit, her back leaning against an empty section of wall. Redd joined her, making sure to angle himself so that he could keep an eye on the Mutants. Sis had placed a heavy chunk of either debris or art—it was impossible to tell which—on the TV Man's head to keep him earthbound, and now she and Buzz quietly conferred with each other in the corner, their voices too low for Redd to make out. That set him on edge again, but Sergeant seemed unconcerned where he waited, watching as Techs did what he could for the TV Man.

Redd didn't envy that challenge. The light from the TV Man's screen flickered through shades of gray as Techs tinkered, though he did seem to calm. Beside Redd, Zero began inspecting her rifle, wiping away the flecks of dirt and other unwelcome matter that it had picked up during their travels. Redd felt himself beginning to calm as he watched her, lulled by the methodical, familiar actions. It had been too long since they'd last done a mission together, he decided. Maybe . . . maybe if they made it out of this mess alive, he could request to be transferred into her squad again. With her in charge, of course. Whether he commanded his own squads or not these days, Zero would always, in a way, be his commanding officer.

She looked up, seeming to sense the somber mood that had overtaken him, lens flashing briefly with a reflection of the TV Man's static. Redd held her gaze before looking away sharply, back out at the room they'd found themselves in. The wall across from them was full of oil paintings, only a few of which had been knocked loose or fallen over the years. Though he couldn't make out as much of the detail or color as he would have liked given the limited lighting, Redd knew that they were beautiful, special in a way that, sometime in the past, had made them worthy of being hung where they were. When he glanced over, Zero seemed to be looking at the artwork as well, maybe even thinking the same thing.

He gave her a thumbs-up. *They're nice, right?*

Zero nodded in agreement. Then she hung her head, as if saddened.

Redd put a hand on her shoulder. *What?*

She looked up, tipping her head toward the paintings again, indicating the gaps between them this time. What remained of what had once hung in those spaces consisted of broken frames and crumpled canvases on the floor below, damaged beyond recognition. But Redd understood that she wasn't mourning their loss. What she was wondering was whether anyone else would ever have a chance to fill those holes back in with something new.

Redd laid down his rifle meaningfully. *This war can't last forever.*

She nodded. *I know.*

What neither of them pointed out was that, when it did end, it was still far from clear which side would come out on top.

Across the room, Techs stood up from where the TV Man's head now sat docilely on the floor, a slightly bewildered but content ~_~ on the screen. The Speakerman reached up to readjust his hat. *"That does it,"* he said. *"Let's—"*

The wall of paintings exploded. The sound was deafening, the force of the explosion hitting Redd like a tsunami. For a moment, he had no idea what was happening, where he was. When the world finally came back into focus, the air was filled with dust and debris. He couldn't make out more than a few inches in front of him, what little illumination there was, it was impossible to attribute to friend or foe. Zero was nowhere to be seen. He flailed, reaching for the space where he thought she'd been a few seconds ago, but found nothing.

Something streaked through the smoke. Redd

jumped back. He got the barest glimpse of what had passed by, but that was enough—a Strider Astro Toilet. It had missed him on the first pass, but didn't on the second, skittering to a stop directly in front of him. Vague shapes moved around in the dimly lit haze behind it, but Redd didn't have time to figure out who—or what—they were. He dove out of the way as the Astro Toilet fired, hitting the wall instead of him, sending chunks of cement and plaster flying. Somehow Redd managed to find the laser rifle he'd set down. He raised it and pulled the trigger. Most of his shots left harmless scorch marks on the Strider Astro Toilet's heavily armored exterior, but one shot struck it directly in the eye. It shrieked and backed off, disappearing into the thick smoke.

Redd was on his feet in an instant and running. It was still nearly impossible to see—what few lights there were had blinked out one by one—and only after he had made it a significant distance without encountering either the others or a wall, he realized he'd gotten turned around. Redd fumbled in his pocket for his flashlight, clicking it on. Ghostly white figures appeared out of the dark. He flinched, but they were simply more statues, this set carved out of bright white marble. What disturbed him more was that he hadn't seen these before, which meant he hadn't passed through this room with the others. He started to backtrack, to try and find his way to where he'd been—where Zero must still be—when he spotted another Strider Astro Toilet through one of the high narrow doorways. He ducked behind a statue, turning off the light as fast as he could. The Astro spun his way a moment later, its searchlight sweeping over the stone figures.

Go away, Redd thought, hoping the Astro would move on. But no such luck. It kept getting closer and closer. Redd watched its light as it swept over the walls and into the far corner of the chamber.

There! He spotted another doorway, not in the direction he thought he wanted to go, but the Astro was nearly on top of him. He waited until it was looking in the opposite direction and made a break for it, moving as fast as he could without giving himself away. The floor suddenly ruptured in a spray of marble chips. It was no use; the Astro had spotted him. Redd spun in place and returned fire wildly, taking the head off a statue but not accomplishing much else except sending the Strider Astro Toilet ducking for cover. It bought him precious seconds though, which he used to slip through the doorway and back into the dark.

Almost immediately he collided with something. It was heavy and unyielding, but also unbalanced, tipping over and crashing to the floor. Redd tried to keep moving, but the pieces of whatever had broken were underfoot and he kept stumbling, colliding with some other large object—which thankfully remained upright—before finding his balance. This was no good. Without light, he'd never get away from the pursuing Astro Toilet, but the flashlight would almost immediately give away his position. He had to make a choice though. He clicked the flashlight back on and ran, hoping to put enough distance between him and his attacker to let him attempt hiding once more. If he could do that, get the Astro as lost in this maze as he was, then maybe he'd have a chance to creep away and get back to where the others were.

If they hadn't moved on by then.

It was a vexing thought, but if they'd managed to regroup, then the decision was clear: keep moving, get to the rendezvous point. He'd been an unexpected addition to their mission anyway; it would be stupid for them to risk failure—and their lives—because he'd been unlucky enough to get separated. No, they wouldn't waste time on him. Zero would know better.

Redd made his way through another chamber and then another, frustration growing as he encountered one that had no exit, and then another whose doorway was blocked by rubble. He must have been moving farther into the center of the building complex though; there were no windows here to offer a convenient exit. Meanwhile, the Strider Astro Toilet drew closer. As quick as Redd was, it remained persistent, unwilling to give up on its prey.

Finally a doorway spilled Redd out into a larger space, a grand hall with more statues and a ceiling high above. He'd come out on a mezzanine in the middle, near a series of marble stairs that led down to another level below. As much as he didn't want to descend deeper into this labyrinth, Redd could see the Strider Astro Toilet's light was nearly upon him. Here, at least, a hole in the ceiling meant he could turn off the flashlight and make use of the moonlight filtering in. Redd shoved the flashlight into his pocket, gripping the rifle tighter as he took the stairs two at a time. There were puddles of water, left by past rainstorms, which he avoided, and patches of slick mildew, which—unfortunately—he did not. Redd's foot caught one of these spots halfway down, his feet going out from under him and sending him careening down to the next level. As he fell, the gun flew from his grip, clattering across the stone with a racket that echoed throughout the hall.

So much for stealth. By the time Redd got himself back up, his pursuer was already upon him, standing on the mezzanine Redd had entered the hall through. And it wasn't alone. Another Strider Astro Toilet had joined it, the one who Redd had blinded in one eye. Its face was filled with particular hatred as he backed away, moving as far from the looming pair as he could. Their three remaining eyes glared from beneath dark helmets. Redd spared a glance at the rifle. It wasn't far away, but the chances of him reaching it before the Astro Toilets were on top of him were . . . well, not great.

The one-eyed Strider Astro Toilet said something in their alien language. The second Astro considered for a moment before the first spoke again, more insistent this time. Finally the second Astro said something that Redd didn't need interpreted: It was agreeing. To what exactly, Redd could guess that too. The one-eyed Astro Toilet had a score to settle with him.

A moment later, it jumped, throwing itself from the level above as Redd dove for the gun, nearly reaching it before the Astro Toilet landed on him. He was knocked to the ground and onto his back, the heavy creature returning quickly as Redd tried to fight it off, pushing and punching and trying to dodge the teeth that snapped at him again and again. One of the mechanical legs jabbed him in the gut; another barely missed skewering Redd right through the lens. Oh, this Astro Toilet was *mad*. No using its mounted weapons to dispatch Redd quickly; it was clearly bent on revenge, and that meant making sure that what it inflicted on Redd was as hands-on—or appendage-on—as possible.

Redd punched again, scoring a glancing blow that caused the Astro Toilet to move back a little, briefly freeing him. But before Redd could take advantage of that, it jumped and landed on him again, its weight nearly crushing Redd. And maybe that was the intention. Smash most of him into bits and pieces, tear the rest apart with its gruesomely oversized teeth. Redd kicked and punched, but with every passing second, he knew it was growing more futile. No matter how hard he fought, this fight was only going to end one way.

Suddenly he heard another explosion. As it echoed through the hall, the Strider Astro Toilet paused in its attempts to dismember Redd, looking back up at where its companion had been observing the fun. That Astro Toilet was gone though. The only evidence left to show where it *had* been was the blood sheeting down the walls of the marble stairs, along with a few unidentifiable chunks. Something stepped forward into its place: Buzz. The Mutant raised his blade-mounted hand, letting it whir menacingly. The Strider Astro Toilet atop Redd grimaced, surprised and confused. But Buzz didn't make any attempt to attack it.

More movement flashed above, and Redd understood why. Sis, on the landing directly above him, was pushing one of the massive statues, which teetered haphazardly. Buzz was the distraction; Sis was the real rescue plan. "Move," she cried as the huge stone visage suddenly gave in to the pull of gravity. Redd pushed the Astro Toilet up with all the strength he could muster, freeing himself just enough to roll out of the way before the statue came crashing down on his attacker. The one-eyed Astro Toilet screamed, a sound that cut off almost instantly as several tons of marble hit it like a foot coming down on a cockroach. Blood and viscera spewed, splattering Redd, but he'd gotten clear in time. Not by much though. The edge of the white stone—red now leaking out from beneath it—was less than an arm's length away.

Redd went limp, head hitting the floor, his lens pointed up at the opening in the ceiling above. For a few seconds, that's as much as he could manage. Then he heard Buzz and Sis making their way down to his level. He forced himself up again, watching warily as they slowly approached. Sis almost looked concerned, but Buzz smiled his unnervingly half-human smile, as if pleased by what they had accomplished.

Why had they saved him? They'd had no reason to. There were no other Alliance members around to see what had happened to him. Even if they'd spotted the Strider Astro Toilets as they'd cornered Redd, the Mutants could have merely stood aside and waited until it was too late. Another dead Cameraman fallen during a war that had claimed so many others . . . No one would have been suspicious, or questioned Redd's fate. The Mutants could have left him to die and been rid of the one member of the team that still questioned their loyalty, freeing them up for whatever they had planned.

But the Mutants didn't let him die. Instead, they killed two Strider Astro Toilets to save him.

"Are you injured?" Sis's concern shifted to cautious relief, though her guard was still up in case another attack came.

Redd shook his head, but the questions kept echoing through his thoughts: *Why, why, why . . . ?*

"Good," said Buzz, satisfied. "You have guts. We need that now." He looked around at the mess left by the dead Strider Astro Toilets and then suddenly burst out laughing. "Or maybe we have enough of those right now."

Lights flashed on the mezzanine again as Zero suddenly appeared above, Sergeant close behind her. They looked like they'd seen some action too, probably left a few dead Astro Toilets in their wake, but also relieved. As soon as she spotted Redd, Zero came running, nearly slipping on the stone the same way he had as she pushed between the Mutants and threw her arms around him.

We thought you were dead, the force of her hug said. *You made it!*

Redd froze at the uncharacteristically sentimental display, one that told him that this time Zero must have really thought he was gone forever. And he nearly had been. The closeness of his demise settled on him with a cold touch, one that was followed by a hint of sorrow. He'd made it out alive again. He couldn't say the same for his squad.

His *former* squad . . . He had a new one now, if only temporarily, and they needed him back in fighting form.

He stood a little taller, extracting himself from Zero, and gave her a thumbs-up. Then with a bit of reluctance still—this was going to take a lot of getting used to—he moved the gesture in the direction of the Mutants. *Thanks. If not for your help . . .*

"We are not out of this yet," Sis said solemnly.

No, they weren't. Someone—well, two someones—were missing. Redd looked around pointedly. *Where's Techs and TV Man?*

Sergeant shrugged with tense aggravation. *Don't know. We got separated, like with you.* He shook his head, pointing in the direction that Redd presumed the river must lie in. *He knows the rendezvous point. We'll have to meet up there.*

Despite his earlier acceptance that the others wouldn't waste time searching for him, Redd bristled. Techs and the TV Man could have simply gotten turned around, wandered into some other part of the building, as he had. But Sergeant was right. It would take too long and be too dangerous to search for their missing companions, especially since they weren't sure how many more of the Strider Astro Toilets were still after them. The immediate threat seemed to have been staved off, but that wouldn't—couldn't—last for long.

"Let's go," said Buzz, leading the way.

This time, Redd fell into formation without argument, not even when Sis took up the rear of their truncated party. They went back up the stairs, exiting the courtyard into another hallway and following it though more of the artifact-littered rooms. There was little point in secrecy now; they moved quickly with lights on, sacrificing stealth for speed. Every moment, Redd expected a fresh round of attacks from another group of Strider Astro Toilets, but somehow they managed to reach another long, open hall without further incident. There they found a welcome sight: windows, one already blown out so fully that they didn't need to bother with the noise of creating an exit. The drop was less than ideal though; nearly three stories separated them from the street below.

"Hold on, we've got this." Sis threw one arm around Zero and the other around Redd. Before he could protest, her grip tightened and she jumped. They landed on the hard ground with a jolt, but safely, Redd stumbling away from Sis as Buzz followed in the same fashion, carrying Sergeant as he leapt from the window to the street. A wide road stretched to either side of them, devoid of movement. But more importantly was what was right in front of them: the river. They'd finally made it to the waterway, which meant they were that much closer to reaching the rendezvous point. Sergeant pointed. Redd could see the ruins of a bridge nearby, but beyond it, in the distance, stood the one that was still intact, the key to their crossing. And despite the Astro Toilet threat that had pursued them through the sprawling complex at their backs, there were still no enemies to be seen.

Sergeant started them moving again, clearly not wanting to waste this window of opportunity. They remained close to the buildings, using the shadows as cover as they made their way toward the bridge. Redd kept scanning the skies and looking behind them; despite the clear path, he was still on edge. It was impossible to shake the sensation that they were being watched, or the reminder that they were now two members of their band short. Wherever Techs and the TV Man were, he could only hope they weren't in danger either.

Sergeant reached the edge of a building and

crouched down, signaling them all to do the same. It was more caution than warning though; the remains of another road cut across their path, leading back into the complex of buildings they'd left behind. Sergeant carefully peeked around the corner of the wall to make sure nothing was lurking just inside the courtyard, but Redd could tell by the way his shoulders relaxed that it was empty. Sure enough, a moment later Sergeant stood again and began to cross—

It zipped into view so quickly that Redd barely had time to realize what he was seeing before the Interceptor Astro Toilet began firing on them. Redd tackled Zero as brick and glass shattered in the space where they'd just been, the Interceptor's plasma guns leaving holes the size of watermelons. Despite the attack, Zero pushed away from Redd and raised her rifle, returning fire. Unfortunately the laser rifles inflicted only glancing damage to the Interceptor's heavy armor, which was even more impenetrable than the other Astro Toilets they'd encountered so far. Sis and Buzz's weapons fared a little better, but even they weren't managing to do much more than keep the attacker at bay. Redd started shooting too, aiming for the Interceptor's soft spots with the intention of blinding it the way he had the Strider, but the Astro

Toilet began to dodge, zipping from side to side, avoiding their shots even as it kept firing upon them. Sis barely missed being hit by a plasma burst that left a smoking hole in the ground beside her. Sergeant, meanwhile, was waving at them to run, knowing that they were outgunned and outmatched.

Redd obeyed but only made it a few steps before the Interceptor shunted itself directly in front of the team with dizzying speed. There was no place to go. To one side were buildings; the other, the river. They couldn't even retreat in the opposite direction. The Interceptor was far too fast for that to be a viable option. There was no choice but to fight and hope that their combined firepower was enough to at least disable the attacker.

Redd glanced Zero's way. It wouldn't be. He knew it, she knew it, and even though they both continued shooting and dodging, it was only a matter of time. Suddenly a laser shot clipped Zero's leg. She went down briefly to one knee before pushing back up and continuing her barrage. Buzz moved his rotating blade in front of his face fast enough to block another blast, but lost a chunk of saw teeth in the process.

"*Heeeeeyyyyy!*" The call, loud and abrupt as it broke through the noise of battle, was so unexpected that

Redd was looking at where it had come from before he realized getting distracted was an easy path to death. He wasn't the only one whose focus had shifted though: Even the Interceptor paused to glance up at where Techs was hanging halfway out of a busted window, waving with one hand, grasping the sack with the TV Man's head in the other.

"*Catch!*" he called to Redd, who was the closest. Redd dropped his rifle and dove to grab the bag as Techs tossed it, catching it just in time. A glimpse within the sack revealed that the TV Man was still okay—or at least as good as he'd been before—a somewhat queasy $\pm\_\pm$ in a field of static staring back at Redd.

The Interceptor spun toward Techs and fired, blowing a chunk out of the building just above the window. Techs was fast though, ducking out of the direct fire and then leaping crazily from the window—not toward the street, but onto the Interceptor itself.

"*Run!*" the Speakerman ordered, one hand holding tight to his hat as the other clung to the Interceptor Astro Toilet, who immediately began trying to buck him off. But Techs held on tight. It didn't matter; he was hardly a match for the Interceptor on his own, even up close. Struggling to keep hold of the TV

Man's bag, Redd went for his rifle again. But Zero stopped him, practically dragging him along as the others took off, Sergeant signaling frantically for them to do so faster.

No. Redd wanted to stop, to turn around and help Techs, but Zero refused to release the grip she had on him. Redd barely managed to look back over his shoulder at where the Interceptor was zipping from place to place, rising higher above the buildings with increasingly frustrated and frantic movements, its unwelcome passenger refusing to be thrown off.

Flush it! Redd thought, directing the notion Techs's way, though surely the Speakerman was trying to do just that. It wasn't as easy with the Astro Toilets as the regular Skibidi Toilets, unfortunately; Techs didn't seem to be having any luck. One hand was stuck keeping hold of the monster beneath him, the other . . .

Redd went cold as the moonlight glinted off something in Tech's hand. Even from a distance, Redd recognized what it was: a detonator.

Oh, that idiot! Techs wasn't only distracting the Interceptor; he intended to . . . Redd looked sharply back at where Sergeant ran ahead of him, desperate to get the leader's attention, warn him about what was about to happen. But Sergeant was already looking back with a sorrow in his countenance that told Redd he was already fully aware of Techs's plan. Sergeant didn't look away either, intent on witnessing the impending conclusion. Redd knew he should turn back too, that it was the least he could do to acknowledge the Speakerman's sacrifice, but—

He heard the sound of the explosion a moment before the force of it hit, nearly knocking him from his feet. Only then did he manage to look behind again, just in time to see the flaming ruins of the Interceptor fall from the sky, smashing into the stone walls that ran along the edge of the river before skipping off them and plunging into the water. Redd's fist tightened. Techs had given his life to buy them all a chance to get away, Mutants included. It had been a wild move, as risky and foolish as they came, but it had worked. Still, even as Redd knew he should be thankful for what Techs had done, all he could picture were the fallen members of his squad. Techs's death was yet another to add to that mental pile, which was growing unbearably high.

A hand smacked him on the shoulder: Zero's. Caught up in grief, Redd had slowed down. The way Zero glared got him moving again. *Don't waste what Techs did,* her look said.

Redd wouldn't. He *couldn't*. Shoving away the vision of the falling wreckage, he concentrated on keeping a grip on the TV Man's bag and putting one foot in front of the other. The space between them and the bridge was narrowing. Then suddenly they were on it, flying across the cobblestones as fast as their legs could carry them. The bridge had seen better days, for sure; there were massive holes where some sort of ordnance had exploded, and a lengthy stretch of the stone rail was long gone, offering only an unimpeded fall into the churning waters below. The river was as dark and foreboding as the city was, and Redd made sure to stay close to the center of the bridge. Then again, the water could offer a quick escape if the Astro Toilets caught them here, more exposed than they'd been thus far. This was the moment they'd worried about. And yet, following what felt like one of the longest minutes of Redd's life, they made it to the other side without a hitch.

On the opposite bank, there was another short stretch of area without cover, but Sergeant rushed them through it and back into the relative safety of the tightly packed buildings. Only there did he signal for them to pause, leading them into the shadows of a destroyed storefront so they could regroup. When they were all inside, Sergeant's shoulders suddenly slumped. He spun and stalked over to the nearest wall, punching it hard enough to leave a hole in the rotting plaster. Redd knew he should do something—knew exactly how the Cameraman felt—but it was Zero who went over, putting one hand on his shoulder calmly. It was a kind gesture, but one that also reminded the leader what they all knew—what they'd all experienced: that this war came with loss. And that at least Techs had gone out on his own terms, in order to save them all.

Sis hung her head respectfully during the exchange.

"We are sorry about your friend," Buzz said simply.

Which was all there was to be said, really. Redd placed the TV Man's head carefully on the floor and took a moment to gather himself.

Sis raised her weapon. "I will keep watch."

Anger flared as she passed by him, headed for the front of the store. *Why couldn't it have been one of the Mutants?* It was a bitter thought, but Redd didn't exactly regret it. The losses added up, each death another one to carry going forward. He knew he could do it, but at this exact moment, the burden felt too heavy, one he wished he could set down as easily as he had the TV Man's head. Redd understood why Techs had done what he'd done, but that barely tempered the sting of the loss. Instead, he tried to focus on his determination, and the goal that they still had a chance to accomplish. They'd made it this far. They could make it a little farther.

According to the map Sergeant had sketched, the rendezvous point was still a fair distance away, and they were beginning to run out of darkness. Which meant they couldn't linger in the shop for long. As they stepped cautiously back into the street, Redd noticed that the night had begun to recede a little, the sky taking on the ebon gray tint that preceded dawn. They picked up their pace, keeping to the narrow streets while avoiding the main thoroughfares, where they'd be more likely to encounter an Astro Toilet patrol. Redd used their stilted movements as a further distraction from the loss of Techs, focusing on darting from doorway to tattered awning to alleyway as they tried to keep out of sight. Given that there were Interceptors around now in addition to the regular Astro Toilet infantry, the biggest threat still came from above.

It was enough to make Redd long for the old days, before most of the Astro Toilets had shown up. In fact, ignoring the presence of the Mutants, this was much like so many other missions he and Zero had been on . . . only deadlier. He repositioned the TV Man's head, shifting the weight so it didn't bang against his back as he ran from one spot to the next, following Sergeant's signals. Again and again they moved, paused, moved and paused again, making more progress in the last half hour than they had during the rest of the night, without spotting a single Astro Toilet in the vicinity. The respite was welcome even as Redd remained suspicious of it. The enemy must be near, so where had they all gone?

Redd could tell by the way Sergeant scanned the area ahead of them with increasing caution that he was apprehensive too. So were the Mutants, who kept looking up at the sky as if they expected an attack at any moment. Only Zero seemed to maintain the cool demeanor he knew so well. Once again, he considered asking for a transfer into her squad if they made it out of here, or maybe even to Sergeant's. There was something here, the beginnings of what could be a first-class Alliance squad, with a little work and some careful recruiting. Spike, for sure, maybe some of their old crew as well. They'd need a good explosives expert too, now that Techs . . .

That thought soured Redd's budding plan. He chided himself for losing focus as well, forcing his attention back to the here and now. If the Astro Toilets cornered them again, he could kiss any chance at that new squad goodbye.

Finally they came to a break in the buildings, a narrow but very long park opening up ahead of them. In the distance, near its opposite end, Redd spotted the huge metal tower he'd caught glimpses of from other parts of the city. Closer up, it had a regal air to it, despite the ruined city surrounding it, almost like a reminder that there was still hope for an end to this war and the alien Toilet invasion.

Sergeant pointed. *That's where we are heading.* He pulled out the beacon and clicked the button. *We're close enough.*

A little of Redd's tension dispersed as the beacon's light began to pulse. All that was left was to get to the rendezvous coordinates where, by the time they arrived, the Alliance would probably be waiting. Just a few more minutes and they'd—

"Watch out!" Sis's warning came in the same instant Redd felt the shift in the air. He dodged to one side, falling awkwardly thanks to the extra weight of the TV Man's head, but it was enough. A charred, smoking hole had appeared where he'd been standing. Suddenly the sky above them was filled with Astro Toilet Interceptors. Five . . . six . . . seven . . . little sonic booms announced the arrival of each as they appeared seemingly out of nowhere, jumping into sight at dizzying speeds.

No. The blossom of hope that had bloomed in Redd quickly withered and died. They'd been so close . . . He turned back toward Sergeant, who gripped the flashing beacon. That explained it—why the Astro Toilets had seemingly backed off after Techs had taken down the first Interceptor. They'd been waiting for the team to get where they were going, where they'd call more of the Alliance into range. A few members of the Camera Faction and a busted TV Man . . . not much of a prize, really, given how many Toilets they'd lost so far. But the forces the Alliance would be sure to send to extract them . . . the TV Faction members who still had their full teleporting ability intact . . .

Redd clenched the sack tighter. Why hadn't they considered this before?

"Traitors," one of the Inceptors growled, the words directed toward Buzz and Sis. "You cannot escape."

"Oh yeah?" Sis laughed mockingly and grinned despite the overwhelming odds. "Bring it on!"

The others raised their weapons, but Redd's had been left behind when he'd taken over possession of the TV Man's head. Not that it mattered. One more laser rifle wasn't going to make a difference, though he'd have felt a little better about all this if he'd been able to join in the last stand the others were preparing to make.

"*.yeH*"

The Interceptor Astro Toilets grinned at them menacingly, amused by the sad attempt at resistance.

"*!yehzzzzZ*"

Redd looked down. The TV Man's bag had slipped open, partially revealing his screen. It flickered pointedly, just enough to get Redd's attention without drawing the Astro Toilets'. Redd moved a little more of the sack aside, revealing an almost coherent :| looking up at him.

"*.em tniopzzzzZ*"

He didn't understand what the TV Man was planning, but they were about three seconds away from death, so there wasn't time for questions. Redd grabbed the head, pulling it out of the sack and angling it up at the Interceptors.

The head began to hum. Suddenly a massive burst of light emanated from the screen, blinding in its intensity and concentrated entirely on the Interceptors. Not expecting the attack, they didn't have time to put on their eye protection. The moment the glow hit them, they flinched but went still, hovering in place but with their eyes frozen open, terror filling them. The burst of illumination only lasted a few moments though; the TV Man's head began to spit sparks again and the light cut off. But the Interceptors remained ensorcelled by its effects.

"*.foO*" the TV Man emitted, his screen back to the gravelly static with a flickering X_X. "*.hcum ooT*"

Redd shoved him back into the bag. Whatever time the assault had bought them, it obviously wasn't going to last long. The others were already running, heading into the park toward the tower. Thankfully there was little here to slow them down. The paths that cut through the overgrown greenery were for the most part clear, and Redd ran like he'd never run before, despite the weight of the TV Man's head. Zero slowed to fall in beside him at the back of the pack. It was appreciated, especially when a scream of frustrated rage sounded behind them, indicating that the TV Man's mesmerizing attack had worn off. She turned and fired at the now pursuing Interceptors, barely needing to slow down to do so.

Redd couldn't do the same, couldn't do anything but focus on what lay before him. The tower grew in size so much more slowly than he liked, the perspective misleading him into thinking the distance was shorter than it really was, but if they could get close enough, Alliance reinforcements could already be waiting, teleported in by—

A plasma blast hit beside them and Redd went airborne. Somehow he managed to maintain his grip on the bag this time, feeling the deep bite of gravel as he hit the ground and rolled. He sat up immediately, hardly caring whether he was in one piece.

Zero? Where was Zero? He spotted her a dozen meters away, trying to shake off the effects of the explosion's shock wave. Luckily she didn't seem to be any more damaged than he was. The blast hadn't scored a direct hit on either of them; if it had, he'd be looking at pieces of her right now. It was a sickening thought, but also as much good fortune as this moment had to offer. The Inceptor Astro Toilets were nearly upon them, the one in the lead swooping down with its weapons locked on Zero.

No. Redd waved his arms as he struggled to get up, to turn the Interceptor's attention toward him instead, already knowing that it was too late to—

As the Interceptor fired, Sis appeared, grabbing Zero and rolling out of the way before the ground where she'd been was turned into a crater. Smoke filled the air, but a hulking form appeared through it: Buzz. With a wild, almost feral shout, he launched himself off the remains of a fountain as the Interceptor reached the lowest point in its arcing path. Buzz collided with the Astro Toilet, sending it lurching unsteadily through the air. Redd heard the high, scraping whir of his saw. A moment later, several pieces—vital ones—went flying from the Interceptor. It spiraled, Buzz leaping from its damaged form before it hit the pavement and exploded. The Mutant had landed near Redd, giving him a manic, satisfied grin as he surveyed his handiwork. Then he turned and began firing on the rest of the incoming Interceptors. Sis was doing the same, holding nothing back as she shielded Zero, who was still trying to get her bearings.

A shadow fell over Redd. It was Sergeant, staring intently as he yanked Redd back onto his feet. *You waiting for an invitation? Let's go!*

Redd obeyed, but shoved the bag with the TV Man's head at Sergeant before darting for Zero. She moved unsteadily, apparently taking the hit harder than he had. Throwing one of her arms around his shoulder, he got her hobbling toward the tower again as the Mutants kept up their suppressive fire. But the Interceptors were all within range now too. Their plasma guns peppered the ground with the intensity of a sudden rainstorm, forcing the team to move in a slower, serpentine pattern to avoid being hit. When Zero stumbled, Redd caught her, but she extracted herself, giving him an unsteady thumbs-up as she started running on her own again.

Redd held out a hand. *Wait!* By now he could tell that she was more than shaken, that she'd taken damage given the way she bent forward a little, favoring her right side. There was no time to assess her injuries though. All they could do was keep moving. Their weapons were gone, their only remaining defense the Mutants behind them. The Mutants that had saved Zero's life—*all* of their lives right now.

Though it seemed as if they would never reach it, suddenly the tower was looming above them, tall as a skyscraper, dawn's light limning the structure in warm pinks and yellows. Beneath it, Redd spotted something that almost made his knees go weak with relief: a telltale cloud of black smoke gathering. A moment later, four figures appeared from out of it—TV Woman, hands on her hips as she assessed the situation coolly, and two Large Cameramen and a Speakerman, all toting rocket launchers. Again Redd nearly fell over as he recognized Spike, his distinctive metal points catching the morning sun in an echo of the tower above. The Speakerman started running at them, waving as one of his favorite guitar riffs screamed from his speaker. Meanwhile, Sergeant had reached TV Woman. He unceremoniously tossed the bag with the TV Man's head into her cloud and started pointing frantically at the Mutants still covering their retreat.

Zero, who was a few steps ahead, looked back to make sure Redd was still there. He started to give her a thumbs-up when suddenly she lunged at Spike, tearing the launcher from his grip before spinning and firing. Redd ducked instinctively, but she hadn't been aiming at him, rather at the Interceptor that had just appeared only a few meters above him. The missile hit it just off center, blowing two of the Interceptor's wings off. It screeched as it spun out of control and crashed, leaving a bloody streak as it skidded across the pavement.

Spike began clapping, but Zero . . . Redd caught

her again as she doubled over, a hand thrown over her middle as she dropped the launcher. Whatever injuries she'd sustained, they were definitely worse than she'd let on.

Bad enough, in fact, that she didn't object when Redd shoved her at Spike and pointed at TV Woman's cloud. *Get her to safety!*

Spike snatched up their former squad leader, carrying her like a child—oh, she was gonna give it to them both for that later—as he tipped his head questioningly at Redd. *"You coming?"*

Redd shook his head and grabbed the rocket launcher. He couldn't, not yet. Turning back to where the Mutants still fought, he raised the weapon and settled it on his shoulder. New allies or old enemies, he couldn't leave Buzz and Sis behind now. He tossed his head at Spike one more time. *Go!*

Spike obeyed, pulling Zero into the smoke and disappearing. Meanwhile, someone had re-armed Sergeant. He and the Large Cameramen were firing at the remaining Interceptors, providing protection for TV Woman, who was just . . . standing there? No, she was looking up, her attention caught by something somehow more compelling than the onslaught of Interceptor Astro Toilets. Redd followed her gaze.

A patch of air near the tower had begun to glisten strangely, bolts of light the color of blood flickering within it.

A massive figure appeared out of the shimmer. Redd froze. Just when he thought the situation couldn't get worse . . .

The placid expression on her face did nothing to offset her terrifying visage, which he'd only seen via recorded feeds before. The Duchess Astro Toilet was a beautiful monster, glowing with the same inevitable keenness as the rising sun as she considered the tiny figures below her. A small smile rising to her lips, she spoke one unintelligible word in the Skibidi language. Immediately the Interceptors ceased their attacks and gathered around her like a flock of terrible birds.

"Ohhh . . ." Her voice was as gentle and cruel as a pillow about to smother someone to death. "Silly creatures. You did not think we would allow this treachery?"

Buzz and Sis had drawn closer together and were backing away toward the tower. Beneath it, TV Woman was hesitating, clearly torn between escaping the deteriorating situation and completing the mission, which came in the form of rescuing the two

Skibidi Mutants still out of reach of her teleportation powers. Redd gripped the rocket launcher and started running for a better position. He needed a clean shot. The Mutants had saved him—saved Zero. It was time to return the favor. He raised the weapon and fired. The noise alerted the two Large Cameramen and Sergeant, who fired as well, all of their missiles streaking directly toward Astro Duchess and her Interceptor entourage. But Duchess was quick. She dodged three of the projectiles before ducking behind an Interceptor who was the unlucky recipient of the fourth. It exploded, scorched pieces of the Astro Toilet raining down.

In response, Duchess screeched, a sound that felt like someone was stabbing an ice pick into Redd's head. Suddenly a force wound its way around him and plucked him off his feet—he was caught in one of Duchess's energy beams, levitating sickeningly several stories off the ground. Then she whipped him around and let go, dispatching him like he was nothing more than a bothersome bug.

This was it, Redd thought as he went flying. A high dark beam came rushing at him. Redd collided with it, the impact rattlingly painful, but he managed to catch an edge of the ironwork, arresting his momentum before he went tumbling over the side. A moment ago, he'd been below the giant tower. Now he was stuck up within it, clinging to the metal framework for his very life. He was so far up that TV Woman and Sergeant looked like a pair of ants, and the Large Cameramen not much bigger. Redd got a leg up on the beam, which was wide enough for him to stand on, just as Duchess turned her beams on the Large Cameramen and Sergeant. Quick on his feet, Sergeant managed to dodge the attack, but the elite Astro Toilet locked on to the others. Their trajectory was less fortunate than Redd's—with a cutting laugh, she tossed them playfully into the air, where the Interceptors quickly finished them off.

It was horrible, but Redd couldn't do anything but watch from where he was stuck. Even if he'd wanted to, climbing down the exterior of the tower would take far longer than they had. Buzz and Sis, beckoned frantically by Sergeant, were running for the teleportation cloud—which TV Woman was holding open for them—but before they could close the distance, Duchess swooped down and fired along the pavement between them, leaving a deep furrow that caused the Mutants to skid to a stop.

Duchess laughed as she hovered just above them,

a sound like glass breaking. "Oh no you don't, little traitors," she said, smiling wider, so that her teeth were showing. "Time for punishment. But first . . ." She swung toward TV Woman and Sergeant, mechanical claws snapping at them. In an instant, they were in Duchess's grip, held tight. TV Woman's teleportation cloud began to thin as she and Sergeant contorted in pain, the metal appendages tightening around them. Meanwhile, the Interceptors laughed.

Redd balled a fist and slammed it against the iron beam beneath him. He couldn't stand being stuck here, forced to watch as Astro Duchess murdered the others. But what else could he do? He was trapped, stories up with no weapons and no way to—

He stood suddenly and reached into his pocket. *Yes!* It was still there, the timed explosive Techs had given him. He'd forgotten all about it. A crazy idea began to come together. Astro Duchess was hovering almost directly beneath him, the cause of his friends' imminent death and all that stood between the Mutants and their chance to deliver G-Toilet's message. If he set the timer, took a running leap . . .

Yes, it could work. The bomb might not be big enough to take Duchess down for good, but with a little luck it would stun her long enough to free TV Woman and Sergeant and clear a path for Sis and Buzz. As long as Redd didn't mind the drop.

Or care about walking away from the endeavor alive.

He squared his shoulders. It had been a good run. And it was poetic in a way, to fall where the rest of his squad had, in this once beautiful city. It had been nice, getting a chance to see Zero and Spike again. He could only hope they wouldn't be too disappointed when he wasn't able to join in the celebration of a mission accomplished.

Redd twisted the timer, pressed the arming button on the bomb, and leapt. It was a long drop, more than it had looked initially, but Duchess was right below, getting closer and closer and—

Suddenly she twisted his way and grinned. Redd's aim was perfect, but instead of her armored exterior, the only thing he hit was an impenetrable energy shield. As smooth and unbroken as a glass globe, there was nothing on it for him to grip, nowhere he could even toss the bomb. Nearby, a whooshing sound began, growing louder as Redd began to slide, falling from Astro Duchess toward the pavement below.

He only had a few brief moments to contemplate his

failure, which was enough for the anger to come rushing in. After everything that had happened—losing his squad, fighting their way through the city, coming to terms with the Skibidi Mutants being allies now instead of enemies—he'd screwed up, not even managing to die in a helpful way.

What a waste . . .

Redd hit back-first. But it wasn't pavement he felt beneath him. If it had been, he would be a pile of parts right now. Instead . . .

He looked up into the colossal, imposing face of Titan Speakerman.

The Titan, who Redd hadn't seen in person since his triumphant disinfection, had caught him. His other hand reached for Redd, fingers deftly plucking the explosive from him and tossing it away. An explosion followed a few seconds later, but Redd barely heard it. The only thing he perceived in that moment was Titan Speakerman, gently closing his hand around Redd's lower half as he landed to one side of the metal tower.

Duchess's pleasant, almost bored expression was gone. She dropped Sergeant and TV Woman, her features twisting with rage as she snarled and snapped something in the Skibidi language. In an instant, the

Interceptors were back in formation and firing on Titan Speakerman, blanketing him with plasma blasts. The Titan twisted around, pulling Redd to his chest protectively, but strangely didn't fight back, even though Redd could feel the hits reverberating through his massive body. Then the growing morning light disappeared briefly as two shadows swept across them. Titan Speakerman straightened as their sources landed, rattling the earth beneath them—Titan Cameraman and Titan TV Man.

All the Alliance Titans, in one place.

Redd would have jumped up and cheered, if he'd been able to.

The Interceptors resumed firing, but Titan Cameraman lunged forward and swiped at the closest before it could get a shot off, sending the Astro Toilet careening away. Then he grabbed a second by the wing, raising it over his head and smashing it against the pavement. The Interceptor shattered like a cheap toy.

Astro Duchess was not amused. She flitted back from the new arrivals, trying to put the tower between her and them, but Titan TV Man was having none of it. He lifted off, matching her movements before stabbing at her with one of his shoulder claws. Duchess barely got her shields up in time, the impact still enough to send her reeling. Meanwhile, Titan Speakerman stood his ground, allowing Redd a chance to see that Sergeant and TV Woman had recovered from the attack. The Mutants had taken the Titans' appearance as an opportunity to reach the pair as well. As Redd watched, TV Woman's teleportation cloud reappeared. Buzz and Sis disappeared into it—to where, Redd had no idea, but at least it would be safe.

Finally. Once they were gone, Sergeant looked up at Redd and popped a thumbs-up. Next to him, TV Woman's screen swiveled from Redd to the cloud with clear indecisiveness. Redd waved his hand frantically at her. *Go! Don't wait for me!*

At first, she hesitated. Then, before Sergeant had a chance to object, she grabbed his arm and disappeared into the smoke.

Everyone was safe. Redd felt himself loosen with the relief of it, all the tenseness that had gathered over this harrowing night finally dissipating . . . only to come back an instant later when an Interceptor suddenly swooped into view, coming at Titan Speakerman from his blind side. Redd slapped at the Titan's hand, hard as he could, drawing Titan Speakerman's attention just in time for him to dodge the Astro Toilet's plasma attack. It swung around for another pass, targeting Titan Speakerman, though from the look of frustration on the alien's humanoid features, Redd was the one it really wanted a shot at. Plasma fire cut a path up the front of the Titan, but he held Redd tight, punching with his free hand. The blow didn't take the Interceptor down, but it did knock it in Titan Cameraman's direction. Titan Cameraman grabbed it, snapping its thruster wings off before smashing the Astro Toilet's face in with a raging fury that even Redd had to turn away from.

Meanwhile, Titan TV Man was still slashing at Duchess. The Elite Astro Toilet tried restraining the Titan with her control beams, but one by one, Titan TV Man broke free of them. Then he braced himself, letting loose a blast from his death screen; Duchess turned away barely in time, throwing up her shields and squeezing her eyes shut. When she opened them again, lifting off to put some distance between her and the Titan trio as she did, anger had turned her features into a furious mask that could never be mistaken for human. She looked around, marking the few remaining Interceptors, not to mention the mangled remains of the ones the Titans had already taken down.

For a moment, it looked like the fight was still on. Duchess's eyes narrowed, as if preparing to fire her optic lasers. In response, the Titans steeled themselves. Titan TV Man flexed his arms, massive claws ready. Titan Cameraman's plasma core flared, and Titan Speakerman emitted a threatening hum as he readied his devastating audio attack. At the sight of this, Astro Duchess backed away farther, not seeming to realize she was doing so until she caught herself. Then, reluctantly, she frowned. "The day is yours." Red energy crackled around her for an instant before she warped away, long gone before any of the Titans could try and stop her. Abandoned, the remaining Interceptors traded several wary glances before doing the same, the skies over the city suddenly entirely clear of Astro Toilets as far as the eye could see.

It was over.

As the Titans basked in their success—trading satisfied looks, a pleased XD appearing on Titan TV Man's screen—Redd leaned back in Titan Speakerman's grip. The Astro Toilets were gone. The battle was over and the Alliance had won. Not to mention he had gotten the chance to witness the combined might of all three Titans, *in person*.

Spike was going to be *so* jealous.

Titan Speakerman looked down at Redd. *"Okay?"* he buzzed.

Redd nodded.

"Good," said the Titan. *"Now we're even."*

Suddenly the Titan's hand lifted Redd higher, placing Redd on his broad shoulder.

"Hold on," Titan Speakerman rumbled.

Redd had only seconds to get a solid grip before all three of the Titans' thrusters began to power up and they launched into the sky. Below, for the first time, Redd got a full view of the city—the ruined but still striking buildings, the river circling in its midst, the long shadow of the metal tower as it stretched over the smoking craters left behind by this latest conflict between the Alliance and the Skibidi Toilets.

No, the Skibidi Toilets were allies now. It still didn't sit right, like a sharp stone caught in his shoe, but Redd had witnessed what Buzz and Sis had done, how they'd fought for him and Zero and Sergeant and not let them become another casualty to add to some Alliance list somewhere. He felt a pang of sadness for the rest of his friends and comrades that had fallen, but they'd done what they came here to do. The Mutants would deliver G-Toilet's message, which would lead to a truce, and—hopefully—the pendulum of war would swing back in their favor again. Maybe, in the not too distant future, cities like this would be able to be rebuilt, the empty spots left by the prolonged conflict filled in. Maybe he'd come here again one day, with his friends . . . with Zero.

As they flew higher, on their way to whatever base the Titans were headed for, Redd began broadcasting. The view was spectacular, something he'd never experienced before and probably wouldn't again. He hoped Zero and Spike would tune in, see what they were missing or, even better, be comforted by the fact that he'd be back with them soon.

ABOUT THE AUTHOR

Lyndsay Ely is the author of the YA genre-bent dystopian Western *Gunslinger Girl,* the Overwatch novel *Deadlock Rebels* and short story "Luck of the Draw," and Five Nights at Freddy's interactive novel *Escape the Pizzaplex.* She spent her teenage years wanting to be a comic book artist but, as it turned out, she couldn't draw very well, so she began writing instead. She is a geek, a foodie, and has never met an antique shop or flea market she didn't like. Boston is the place she currently calls home, though she wouldn't mind giving Paris a try someday.